Following
Chance

CHAPTER ONE

I never thought I would be back in Renfrew after a fifteen-year absence, pulling a number of carefully organized boxes out of a U-Haul. Boxes for the bedrooms, the bathrooms, and kitchen, but no box for my sanity or lack thereof. The search for stability involved uprooting my life and my daughter's because I was burned out. It was selfish, but I was out of options. The better parts of me were absent and usually found in the confines of my office when they should have been as a parent and a person. Something had to give. I scrutinized our savings account with a fine-tooth comb and determined that even with the move and the career change, we would be just fine. We had to be.

It took a few days for my daughter, Jack, to adjust to our new surroundings, but I had no doubt she would, as she was the strongest person I knew. She was accustomed to the hustle and bustle of the city, and up until that point in her life, she didn't realize that things could move at a much slower pace. I was already well versed in the pregnant pause that was this small town because I had spent my college years here. There was the downtown, the college, a handful of businesses, but not much else. Older homes surrounded the river and the newer homes that had been built in the last century occupied First through Fifth Street. You could drive around the entire city in twenty minutes or less. Jack would be able to ride her bike anywhere she pleased. She never would have done that in the city, not with the cars, busses, and pedestrians jockeying for position; they never would have given a second thought to my ten-year-old.

In a week, I would be starting my new job, replacing Ms. Houtby, as the Humanities purchaser for the college library. It was like coming home again and I knew that the same smells that greeted me on my first day of college would still be present like they had never left. Reliable. Dependable. Home. *Why did I ever leave?* The truth was, I wasn't replacing Ms. Houtby, I was returning to a career that I had left fifteen years earlier. I was on the precipice of starting my life, or starting my life over...I couldn't decide which. But at the moment, I was on the verge of sorting the last remaining boxes in our garage and it felt like a small victory.

"Mom, can I ride around the block?" Jack broke me from my thoughts. She had helped for the last thirty minutes and then ridden her bike up and down the driveway.

"I don't know..."

"Please? I know where I'm going."

"We've only done the route a couple of times."

"I promise I'm not going to get lost."

Deep down I knew that she wouldn't as she had a better sense of direction at ten then I did at thirty-seven. "Okay...but if you aren't back in twenty minutes, I'm sending out a search party." She maneuvered her bike, ready to race into the street. "I won't be thrilled to be leading it!"

"Twenty minutes," she called over her shoulder.

"I'm timing you!" I called out just as she departed.

"I know!"

I turned my attention back to the boxes, but not more than a minute later, I heard the tires of a bicycle come to an abrupt stop just short of the garage and a little bell rang out.

"Jack, I didn't say twenty seconds..." But when I turned around it wasn't Jack, but her doppelgänger in a yellow sundress riding a pink bicycle.

"Do you have a daughter?"

"I do." I smiled at her directness and looked down the street, but Jack was long gone. "She just went for a ride around the block."

Jack 2.0 looked distinctly disappointed. "My mom won't let me do that yet..." She looked down the street and my gaze followed. A woman, no doubt her mother, was making her way up the sidewalk toward my house.

I turned my attention back to the young girl. "She'll be back soon if you want to meet her. What's your name?"

"Abbie."

She couldn't have been older than Jack. She had long, light brown hair and a pair of bluish-green eyes that looked sweet and oddly familiar. She was a pint-size version of me minus the sundress. Thankfully, my mother could never hold me still long enough to capture me in one.

"I'm Jack's mom. You can call me Kate."

"Jack?" she asked confused. "That's a funny name for a girl."

"It's short for Jacquelyn. She hasn't let me call her that in years. She goes by Jack."

"*Abbie!*" a voice called out from the sidewalk and I immediately froze.

Fuck. I closed my eyes and counted to ten. It couldn't be her. I turned to the bottom of my driveway with my breath trapped in my lungs. When my eyes found hers, I thought I had seen a ghost. *Lauren.* The word boomed throughout my entire body, but never materialized into sound. My heart started to beat frantically, causing a dull pain. "She was just asking about Jack..." The words slipped quietly from my lips, and the green eyes that were focused on Abbie immediately shot up and found mine.

She blinked with her head tilted slightly to the side.

I screamed at myself for not putting the pieces together quickly enough to send Abbie on her way, so that I could return to the safety of my home.

She shook her head like she was clearing the cobwebs and studied me carefully. The second the blood drained from her face, I realized she had made the connection. "You grew your hair out."

I had thought about seeing Lauren again a hundred million times and not in a single scenario were her first words to me after fifteen years about my hair. I winced and brushed the locks behind my ears. *Out of sight, out of mind.* But it was no use as her gaze was fixed and not retreating anytime soon. She looked like she had been hit by a sixteen-wheeler. At that moment, I too felt the jarring impact. I did everything in my power to keep myself as even and calm as possible. "So…you don't let her ride alone yet?" I asked stupidly, shrugged and looked for anything to do with my hands which had started to flail wildly out of control. I shoved them into my pockets and pressed my lips together.

"Kate–"

I held up my hand, not wanting to hear anymore from a voice that had haunted me for years. "I didn't know that you were still in town…" I trailed off from the shock, but recovered enough to utter, "Don't worry. I lost your number a long time ago."

"Well, it looks like I have your new address…" My stomach bottomed out as she surveyed the house, no doubt lost in her own shock. "What are you doing back in town?"

And although I wanted to say nothing and bolt for the front door, my manners took over. "I took a job at the library."

"The library?" The disbelief blossomed but before she could ask any other questions, she was interrupted.

"How do you know my mom?"

I looked down at Abbie, not wanting to answer, but what other choice did I have? "We went to school together."

"Then you know my dad?"

A simple innocent question that deserved a simple innocent answer. "I do." I tried to force a smile, but I just couldn't do it. I could feel Lauren's presence, her eyes, the thousand questions she wanted to ask, even though I said nothing. I tried to keep my gaze focused on Abbie, but I did a quick check down the sidewalk to see if Drew was in tow. Thankfully, he never materialized.

"You're very inquisitive, you know that? You're just like my daughter."

"You have a daughter?" Lauren couldn't hide the surprise in her voice.

"Jacquelyn."

"She goes by Jack," Abbie added, and I finally smiled, although it felt uneasy.

"How old is she?" Lauren fumbled with the words, which she never did.

"Ten going on twenty-five. She wants to be a pirate when she grows up," I added for Abbie.

"*Really?* Wow…"

"I know. I hope it happens. It would be fun to have a pirate for a daughter. What do you want to be when you grow up?" I rambled because it didn't look like either one of them had any intentions on leaving my property anytime soon. I quickly looked down at my watch. I should have told Jack ten minutes and then I could have ended whatever the hell this was.

"A scientist that helps animals." Broke me from my thoughts. Abbie practically jumped at the idea and it was so unlike her mother. Had Lauren been this way when she was Abbie's age? Or was this Drew's influence, or a combination of the two of them? I wondered, but I never asked.

"Maybe you and Jack can team up and be marine biologists," slipped out because, although I could find somewhere to put my wayward hands, I couldn't find anywhere to put my words.

"Can I, Mom?"

I could feel Lauren's eye roll, but I didn't dare look back to meet her gaze.

"We've got to get going, Abbie. Say goodbye."

Abbie stuck her hand out at me and the gesture shocked me into inaction. That wasn't Lauren, and it certainly wasn't Drew. It was me, but it couldn't possibly be. She probably saw it in a movie once and thought it was charming and decided to run with it. I looked down at the small extended hand and finally took it in mine and shook it, just firm enough to let her know that I was taking her seriously. "It was nice to meet you, Abbie."

She released my hand and maneuvered her bike in the direction of her mother. When I looked up, I got a split-second glimpse of Lauren's face before she walked off with Abbie. She looked exactly how I felt at that moment, completely pulled apart.

CHAPTER THREE

A few weeks after we were settled and most of the house was sorted, I closed my bedroom door and pulled out a box from under my bed. It was marked *Miscellaneous* and seemed to follow me around with every change in address. Four moves in fifteen years. I had become somewhat of an expert at packing up my life into a number of carefully marked boxes and moving them around. A restlessness that fit into 18 x 18 x 16 square inches.

I brushed my hand over the red lid, wiping away the dust that had accumulated. It had been a while since I took a trip down memory lane. The items at the very top were my most treasured possessions. I picked up Jack's adoption certificate and a small scrap of her baby blanket and smiled. I never thought that I would be a mother. More than that, I never thought I would do it solo. When a colleague went through the adoption process, I found myself asking question after question, until I was sending out emails and enrolling in courses. Everything before that day was a blur of work and women, but after the adoption, Jack became my purpose. As for the keepsakes hiding just underneath, they should have been thrown out years ago. Those items had no business being in my life anymore, yet I couldn't bring myself to part with them. I wanted to forget, but given that they were always underfoot, I knew I never would. I pulled out a small journal with cards and various notes stuck between the pages. I absentmindedly flipped through the blank sheets, but I knew where I would arrive, as I always ended up at the same spot. It was the reason that I stretched along the floorboards and reached for that damn box in the first place. I pulled out a card made of green construction paper with a note scribbled on the inside.

Sometimes i call to ask about school… just so i can hear your voice.

My fingertips traced over the half-cursive, half-print script. I had memorized every curve, to the point that I could pick it out of a police lineup, if half-cursive, half-print ever committed a crime and they needed me to identify the perpetrator. I'd point to the decapitalized i's that dominated her writing. "Yes, officer, that's the one." I'd nod my head fervently. "That's the one that's haunted me all this time…"

My finger fell to the second line and I traced out the name.

Lauren

I held the card to my nose and inhaled deeply. The day she slid it across my desk, she sprayed it with her perfume. It was intoxicating. Lavender mixed with something else. For months, even years after, I was convinced that I could still smell her fragrance mingling with the decaying construction paper. After all this time, the smell had completely vanished, but my memory and senses filled in the blanks and I was instantly taken back to the night we met. I closed my eyes and let myself linger on the memory for a moment. I didn't have much from my time with Lauren, hardly anything, just a bottomless pit of emotions that I could never seem to climb out of and that little card bathed in her perfume.

I also had hidden a box in my mind. Into it had gone every last memory of our time together in college. I'd taped it shut and marked it *Fragile—Contents Will Kill You*, in big block letters on all sides. I'd taken that box to the deepest ocean in my mind and let it sink to the very bottom. I figured that given enough time, the fish would take care of it. I was wrong. I should have burned it. It's funny the things that float to the surface, especially the ones that cause us pain.

* * *

Jack's first day at her new school was more nerve-racking for me than it was for her. The urge to make sure she fit in and make friends kept me up most of the night, even though I knew it didn't faze her. She needed very little to be happy, but I wanted so much for her. Moving back to Renfrew allowed us that, but more importantly it gave us the quality time together that we wouldn't have had in the city. I associated my tiny college town with an easier way of life, and I wanted to give that to my daughter. I had experienced it firsthand during my college years and the novelty never wore off. It was charming. As much as I loved it the first time around, I had to leave it behind to pursue a different life in the city, a life that I thought I wanted.

When Jack arrived as a toddler, those lights quickly faded and the life that I had built post-Lauren couldn't coexist with my responsibilities as a parent. But in my pursuit to ensure that Jack had the best of everything, it meant longer hours at the office. We both needed more, quantity and quality.

Today was the first day that Jack wouldn't have to take public transit to school. We could walk hand in hand down the streets and be at her school. She let me hold her hand to the halfway point and then gave my fingers a squeeze and put both of her hands on her backpack straps. She was becoming more independent with each passing year, but she'd always been that way, even at a very early age. When we arrived at the school yard, she stopped me before I could pass the threshold of the playground.

"I got this, Mom." She looked up at me brimming with a confidence that I never possessed at her age. If this was the city, Jack would have taken the subway from our condo and travelled two stops to get to her school. Walking to school together would be completely out of the ordinary for us, but I welcomed the change, and I didn't want to part just yet.

"I know you do, sweetheart, but just humor me for today, okay?" I put my hand on her shoulder and we walked into the school. I introduced myself to the principal and her teacher, but I didn't stay much longer, as I needed to get to my first day at the library. I gave her a quick kiss on the top of her messy blond head and was on my way.

When I arrived at work, it didn't take me long to find my desk. I pulled a number of items out of my bag—a picture of Jack and me, my white ceramic mug with an image of a little ghost, a Christmas gift from Jack, and a miniature cactus. I turned on my computer and logged into the system. Despite the online tutorials that I had been working on over the past few weeks, I knew that it would take the better part of the day to try and get up to speed.

At three thirty my messy pirate walked into the library with her bag slung over her shoulder like she owned the place. She offered a silent wave and sat down in the empty seat across from me.

"How was your first day of school, baby?" I half whispered so that we wouldn't disturb the students working on their research.

"Awesome, I love my teacher."

I leaned across the desk and gave her arm a gentle squeeze. "That's great. Did you make any friends?" It was something that I was always concerned about, as Jack kept to herself, despite my encouragement.

She leaned back in the chair and a huge smile crossed her face. "I met the most amazing girl today." I beamed and she continued. "She sits beside me in class. She's so nice and smart, and we hung out at lunch." Jack swooned a little and I was a bit taken aback at the gesture.

"Oh?" I continued to study her expression. "That's wonderful. What's her name?"

"Abbie," she whispered excitedly.

My stomach bottomed out. "Abbie?" I swallowed. "Do you know what her last name is?"

"Dawson," she said dreamily.

I closed my eyes and shook my head.

CHAPTER FOUR

Fifteen years earlier

I pushed the book trolley down the carpeted corridor, picking up discarded books as I went. I turned a corner and pushed the cart against the end of one of the stacks, grabbed a pile of books and walked into the middle of the row to start re-shelving. I was lost in the numbers on the spines when a women's voice called out behind me, "Can you help me find a book?"

When I turned, Lauren stood at the end of the stack with a scrap piece of paper in her hand and a smile on her face. As she made her way toward me, my heart immediately slammed into my rib cage, desperate to escape, but got stuck in the gaps, like an exuberant puppy not thinking through the logistics and getting trapped in the doggy-door.

"This is my third time trying to find you. I almost thought you lied to me," she said as she approached, coming within feet of me, no concern for my personal space. Perhaps she ignored that lesson in kindergarten.

"Why would I do that, Lauren?" I shrugged nonchalantly as an unfamiliar voice called out from the recesses of my mind. *Back away from the married woman.* I took a step back until we were standing at a more comfortable arm's length. In the process, her gaze darted down to my feet and she gave me a quizzical look.

"You remembered my name."

I nodded but said nothing as I was desperate not to blurt out, "hard to forget."

"Can you help me find something?"

When she handed me the scrap of paper there was an internal pang of regret. This wasn't a social visit. She merely needed help. I gave myself a mental shake and looked down at the call number and then back up at her. "You're on the wrong floor. Don't you know the Dewey Decimal System?"

She scrunched her eyebrows together. "The what?" She looked genuinely mystified.

"The system that keeps all of the books in order so that you can approach me and ask for my help and I actually know how to help you. Your book is on the fifth floor." She continued to look at me blankly. "Are you for real?" I almost laughed but held it back when she looked down at her feet in embarrassment. "How have you gotten through college without knowing this?"

"I usually get online journals or reserve a book so that it's waiting for me at the front desk."

I released a half-snort, half-laugh. "How very *Princess and the Pea* of you. Well, you're long overdue on some legwork. Here, I'll show you."

We walked up to the fifth floor in silence. *Why did you come back three times to look for me when you could have asked any of the other staff members to help you find this book?* I took another look at the number and beelined between the stacks until I pulled the book from the shelf. "What's the book for?"

"A paper due in a couple of weeks."

I handed her the book and there was an awkward silence. "Good luck with your paper."

As I moved past her, she quickly uttered, "I'm sorry about the other night."

I stopped and turned.

"I think I could have said something better than, 'Oh.'" She cradled the book against her chest.

"It's okay. You didn't run away or say something homophobic. I can deal with surprise."

There was a lull in the conversation and as I was about to head back downstairs, she blurted, "Are you dating a woman?"

Apparently, I wasn't the only one who was prone to foot in mouth disease. Unfortunately, she had probably picked it up from me. I was never going to another party again.

"Are we really back on this subject?" I didn't want to get into my personal life with someone I barely knew, but I felt if I didn't throw her a bone, these questions would never cease. "I'm not dating anyone. Not a man, not a woman, not a crowned head of Europe who just needs my help with some shipping containers."

My last comment eased some of the tension and she smiled.

"How come you aren't dating?"

"It's a small campus. There aren't that many women to date and the others just haven't figured out the joys of being with another woman yet, but they will." I added a wink for emphasis.

"Oh."

There was that word again, hanging between us. It was impossible not to notice how her mouth pushed yet held the sound. "You say that word a lot. I don't want to date someone just to date."

She considered me for a long moment while she smiled. I allowed the quiet observation. "When does your shift end?"

I looked down at my watch. "A couple more hours."

"Swing by the Steam Bean before you go home."

"Why?"

"Because." She smiled as she walked past me and added, "I'm asking."

"Why?" I called out again, but no response came.

She turned down the aisle and walked away.

I silently reprimanded myself for how long my gaze lingered at the end of the aisle, hoping that she would reappear.

Despite my better judgment, I walked across the street when my shift ended. Lauren didn't see me at first as there was a line of impatient students waiting for their afternoon caffeine fix. When she noticed me standing next in line, I was convinced that it was the first genuine smile that she had given a customer in the last five minutes. "Hi," I offered lamely, as I adjusted my worn messenger bag over my shoulder.

"You came." She wiped her hands on a clean cloth.

I shrugged and my smiled faded when I remembered she was married. I quickly glanced at the chalkboard. "I thought I could grab something to drink and review some case studies before I go home. What's good?"

"Is this your first time here?"

"No, but I just usually make instant at home."

The truth was that I couldn't justify the cost of the often overpriced and underwhelming coffee that existed at most chains. My instant coffee was reliable. I knew exactly what to expect and I was rarely disappointed.

Unfortunately, Lauren didn't feel the same as she scrunched up her face in complete disgust. "Can I surprise you with something?" She reached for a white and blue cup.

"I'm not crazy about surprises…"

"I promise, you'll love it." The words were off her lips and she was already reaching for a number of different canisters.

"How much?" I pulled out some cash and tried to pass it to her, but she ignored my outstretched hand completely.

"My treat." She turned from me and reached for a bottle.

"Don't be silly." I was never going to let her pay for my coffee, straight woman or not. I had never let another woman pay for me and I wasn't going to start now. It was a weird kind of feminist-lesbian-chivalry that I wouldn't concede to anyone.

"I'm not."

When she refused to take my money, I put the bills into the tip jar.

"*Kate*." She scowled at me like I had just offended her dignity.

"*Lauren*," I mock-whined in response. "I hope your creation lives up to the tip."

"Grab a seat and I'll bring it over when it's done."

I found an empty table and pulled out my books. I started to scan my last case study, a fascinating decision from the 1930s about ginger beer and snails. I was engrossed in the nuances of the language when she pulled out a chair and sat down. When I looked up, a steaming cup was in front of me. My name was written in neat cursive writing with an exclamation mark at the end and an upside-down heart instead of the period. My gaze lingered on the little heart. I desperately wanted to look at other takeout cups in the shop to see if I was the only one lucky enough for the gesture. I shook the thought from my head as the smell from the cup hit my senses. "It smells delicious. What is it?"

"Guess."

She gently pushed the cup toward me and again it felt like she was unaware of the societal rules of personal space. I took a tentative sip.

"Well?" She leaned forward slightly in her seat.

"It's coffee and chocolate and…" I closed my eyes, took another sip and tried to place the last flavor.

"It's a chocolate-vanilla latte, but there are a couple of other things in there."

"Amazing." I opened my eyes.

She beamed at the compliment. "Just something I've been working on."

"You should get them to put it on the menu." I took another sip. "How do I tell them how to make it, if I come in one day and you're not here?"

She tilted her head. "You can't have it then," she teased, but the look in her eyes suggested that both sound and sight were coconspirators. It felt more than a little dangerous.

"I can't?" I bit down on my bottom lip to suppress the grin.

"Nope. It's a you and me thing."

"We have a *thing*?" It was my turn to tease and I instantly regretted it when her face flushed just slightly.

Damn it. I was blatantly flirting with the married straight woman. I internally slapped myself upside the head.

CHAPTER FIVE

After the news of Jack and Abbie's friendship, it wasn't long before I started seeing Lauren pop up everywhere. It was a relatively small town, but this seemed unusual for Renfrew. I first noticed her during our morning routines. Lauren would drop Abbie off at school at approximately the same time I dropped off Jack. Lauren and Abbie always walked together hand in hand right up to the main entrance doors. When we arrived, Jack would give me a quick hug and be off. A moment later, Lauren would give Abbie a hug and a kiss on the cheek and she would make her way into school. My voyeuristic morning routine only lasted forty-five seconds, but in those brief moments, Lauren captivated me after all this time. Her hair was a little darker than before. Her eyes were just as green. Her lips… My fingertips would always twitch wanting to reach out and touch them, which forced me to push my hands into my pockets.

I never approached her and she never approached me. We kept our distance. We both had become experts at it for the last fifteen years, and there was no reason to change now. Sometimes she gave a small nod in my direction and because I wasn't raised in a barn, I would also nod back an equal amount of times.

I looked forward to our morning nods. It started to feel as natural as the caffeine in my coffee. They were an acknowledgment of the other's existence—nothing more, nothing less—and it was enough. When our paths didn't cross for whatever reason, I felt the withdrawal. My heart, although completely fractured, still remembered Lauren. It beat a little faster in her presence, perhaps it always would despite the pain that she was so inexplicably tied to.

If I wasn't seeing Lauren at Jack's school, then it was at the market on Saturday, the grocery store on Sunday, or to and from work. It wasn't long before I realized why Lauren seemed to be everywhere that I roamed. I learned through some of my colleagues that she had purchased the Steam Bean a couple of years back and was running the place. As soon as I heard the news, I avoided it at all costs, as there was no way that I could successfully order my favorite cup of coffee through a series of nods. Her purchase of the Steam Bean confused me to no end. From the short amount of time that we spent together in college, I knew that it wasn't what she wanted to do with her life. Sure, she loved the shop, but she had plans to travel and write. After I left Renfrew, I spent more than a few sleepless nights wondering how all of her plans had unfolded over the years. When I heard that she was the new owner, the sleepless nights returned. Had her plans unraveled or evolved over the years? Every time that I saw her in town, I had a new question that I wanted to ask, in order to sort the pieces of the puzzle, but I couldn't bring myself to contribute anything further than a nod.

* * *

It didn't take long for Jack to come down with her first cold after we were a month into the school year. She was never susceptible to them before, but given the changes in both of our lives, I wasn't the least bit surprised when it happened. I kept her home for the day, took my own sick day and made her all the things that I knew would make her comfortable: homemade chicken soup, fresh bread, and hot chocolate. On days like these, there was hand holding and snuggling, and she never once reached for her backpack straps. An absolute suck when she was sick, just like her mother, even if no genetic markers indicated such.

As I was puttering around the house, late in the afternoon, the phone rang. I didn't think to look at the number as I fumbled with a pair of mismatched socks.

"*Hellooo?*" I said oddly as I reached for a sock that had fallen out of my grip.

"Hi, Kate. It's Lauren." Her voice floated across the line.

Did she honestly think that I had somehow forgotten? Impossible. She could have called me one hundred years from now and I still would have recognized that voice. The problem was that at that moment, I couldn't find mine.

"We didn't see you two today…"

There have been thousands of days that you haven't seen me, but you didn't pick up the phone to call.

"When Abbie came home from school, she mentioned that Jack wasn't there. Abbie wanted me to call to make sure she was okay."

Hadn't we been running along smoothly without any conversation so far? I was living perfectly well with our morning nods. There was a balance to that existence. I knew that I would see her for exactly forty-five seconds and then she would head down one street and I would meander down another until she was safely tucked away in her coffee shop and I was inside the library. Hadn't that been enough excitement? I came to the sudden realization that it wasn't a cold Jack had contracted, but a curse. It was the only way to explain this phone call. I said the only thing I could think of at that moment. "How did you get our number?" The question squeaked out of me like a rusty door.

"I think Jack must have given it to Abbie. She had it written in her agenda."

"*Oh.*"

As soon as Jack recovered from this cold, we were going to have a very frank and direct conversation about which girls we gave out our number too, especially if those girls had any six degrees of separation from my own past. I didn't want to speak with Lauren. I couldn't speak to her. It wouldn't go anywhere good, no matter how hard I tried to be reasonable and rational, as our time in college had severely stunted my emotional maturity.

"May I please speak with Abbie?" I asked as nicely as I could.

"Sure…"

The phone was muffled for a second and then an unsure, "Hi," came softly from the other end.

"Hello Abbie," I said sweetly, easing her into a conversation that she had just been thrust into. "It's Kate Connors, Jack's mom. How are you?"

"I'm good, Ms. Connors."

"You can call me Kate. It's okay."

"How's Jack?" she asked, the second the formalities were out of the way.

"She's got a bit of a cold. I think I'm going to keep her home from school tomorrow as well. I don't want her getting you sick."

"Okay," she said in a disappointed tone.

"It's for the best, but maybe you could do a huge favor for Jack."

"I'll do anything for Jack," she said quickly.

I sighed internally at what was starting to become crystal clear. "I know you would. Can you pay attention really well in class tomorrow so that you can tell Jack what she missed while she's away from school?"

"I can!"

"I knew you could do it. Jack's always telling me how smart you are. Have a good night, Abbie. If Jack's feeling better, I'll send her to school on Wednesday."

"Can I call tomorrow night to check?"

I sighed internally. "Of course, you can call anytime you want."

"Good night Ms. C–…Kate," she said and handed the phone back to Lauren.

"Kate?"

I didn't say anything. I waited for her to hang up but she didn't. She held onto the phone and cradled the silence. I didn't know what I wanted to say and I couldn't nod the words over the phone. I did the only thing that I could think of. "Good night, Lauren." I didn't wait for her reply. I hung up.

It was our first real unforced conversation in fifteen years and all things considered, I thought that I handled it reasonably well. I was still intact, even though my insides pulled on me like a riptide. I knew that I would repeat and replay every single word that was exchanged between us for the remainder of my evening; there would be no more sock sorting.

CHAPTER SIX

Fifteen years earlier

I pushed the trolley through the aisles of the basement. This was both my favorite and least favorite floor of the library. It housed the advanced science and biology books, which interested me, but there were always a thousand of them to put away. I absolutely loved it because the layout was a convoluted maze of nooks and crannies that I could disappear into for hours at a time. I parked beside the biology section, grabbed a stepstool and sat in a nook while I flipped through a volume on human anatomy. The words were completely above my comprehension, and I could barely string two of them together, but the pictures looked fascinating.

"I thought I'd never find you," Lauren called out from down the aisle, breaking me from my fascination. "Shouldn't you be working?"

"I technically am. I'm restocking and making sure the Dewey Decimal System is in order. I was just taking a break to flip through this." I held up the book.

"You have to make sure it's all in order? Oh my God, that's… What's the suicide rate for librarians?"

"I have no idea." I laughed. "It's tedious, but it's part of the job description. We do a little bit at a time. You'd be surprised how many students hide books in the stacks so that they have exclusive access to them. For the last two years, someone had hidden a book on the third floor. It's supposed to be on the fourth floor and sticks out like a sore thumb if you know what to look for. Every week I put it back and a couple of days later it ends up on three. I've left messages inside to the book bandit, but I never get a response."

"What have you written?"

"Who are you? I know what you're doing. Why won't you think of the other patrons who may need this book? It feels like a game. I really don't want to catch them; it's too fun."

"Who knew the library could be so quirky?"

"Not to mention the dozens of places to make out."

"Oh really? Personal experience?" She wiggled her eyebrows.

"I wish. There are at least ten good spots on every floor, but the basement," I looked down my nook for emphasis, "there's at least thirty. I'll show you sometime." I winked.

She blushed and looked away.

Why was I flirting with this woman?

"What does your second semester look like?" she asked.

It was an odd question considering it was more than two months away. "Pretty good. Mostly legal theory, but I had room for an elective so I'm taking Women's Twentieth-Century Literature on Monday afternoons."

"You are?" She tilted her head.

"Don't seem so surprised. It's the only way I can force myself to read something half decent. Otherwise, it's case studies until graduation. What does your semester look like?"

"Nothing exciting, my pre-thesis for grad school."

I put the volume back and glanced at the clock on the wall. "Don't you start work soon?"

She looked down at her watch—a thick oxblood leather strap with a brushed silver face. I remembered noticing it on our very first introduction as it seemed somewhat out of place against her wrist. "Are you going to pop by the shop after work?"

"I wasn't planning on it."

"Come by for a few minutes and keep me company. It's going to be slow today with the long weekend. I'll treat you to a latte."

"I'll treat you to a tip."

"One of these days can't you just let me do something nice?"

"Not today." I smiled. "You better get going. I'll stop by when I'm done."

"You better."

CHAPTER SEVEN

Leftovers put away, check.
Jack's lunch packed, check.
Garbage by the curb, check.

I went through the mental checklist in my head as I stared blankly at the paperback resting in my hands. Jack chose that moment to run into the living room and fling herself over the arm of the sofa, *Dukes of Hazzard* style, and plopped down beside me.

"Mom," she rushed out.

"Yes?"

"Abbie and I want to have a sleepover."

I cringed inwardly and then outwardly because I wasn't made out of steel. I quickly tempered it for Jack's sake. "Why?" I asked cautiously. I grabbed my bookmark and set the book aside. Reading time was over.

"She's my best friend. That's what best friends do. Samantha slept over at Sophie's last weekend. I want Abbie to sleep over here."

"And if Sophie asked Samantha to buy methamphetamines, would you want to do that too?"

"What?" Jack asked clearly confused.

"Never mind." I pinched the bridge of my nose. It wasn't my proudest parenting moment. "It's not only up to me. Abbie's mother also has to agree."

"She is. Abbie's going to ask her tonight. *Well?*" Jack looked at me expectantly. "Can we?"

"You guys only just met. What do you even know about her?" I said offhandedly.

"She sits beside me in class. Her middle name is Caroline. She always shares her snacks with me. Her parents are divorced," Jack rambled on, but the last word caught my attention.

"Her parents are divorced?"

"She sees her dad every other weekend, well…*sometimes*. Abbie's dad and stepmom have a new baby."

Stepmom? The blood rushed between my ears and a thousand questions popped up in my mind. "I'm sure it's just a temporary thing if there's a new baby. That's too bad," I said after a beat.

"That's why we wanted to ask about this weekend because next weekend she has to see her dad."

"I don't know." I hesitated, but I couldn't think of one good reason to deny the request of my ten-year-old.

"*Mom*," she whined, her hands palms up like she was pleading.

"*Jack*. What did I tell you about whining?"

"That it's annoying." She changed her tone and folded her hands together. "Please?"

I looked heavenward and sighed. Surely, this was the universe getting a big laugh at my expense. It was my own damn fault for coming back. Karma worked in mysterious ways.

"Okay, Jack. If Lau—" I caught myself. "If Abbie's mom says it okay, then she can stay."

Jack threw her arms in the air and fell back on the couch. "Thanks, Mom! You're the best."

CHAPTER EIGHT

Fifteen years earlier

No matter how hard I tried I couldn't seem to keep myself from the shop during Lauren's shifts, even though I knew that my instant coffee was not just reliable but infinitely safer. Similarly, Lauren kept popping up at the library, when she could have and should have been somewhere else.

"You're going to get me into trouble one of these days." I pointed down at Lauren whose back was pressed up against a stack of books as she helped me scan the spines. This was one of the necessary evils of a Saturday morning at the library, when it was quiet enough that only the most boring and monotonous tasks could be accomplished uninterrupted.

"How are you possibly going to get in trouble with me sitting here?"

"This isn't a two-person job. It's a one-person job for the person who is getting paid to do it. Besides, what happens if you do it better than I do and they find out? Then they'll want to hire you and fire me and that can't happen. I need this job."

"Do you want me to leave?" she asked, sounding a little hurt.

"No." I sighed. "I'll just lie if upper management comes around. I'll say that you've fallen, hit your head, can't get up and decided to start sorting books. Stranger things have happened. I don't want you to leave." *Never.* My mind reeled as I tried to bring my attention back to the task at hand. I wanted to ask her a thousand questions, but I kept getting stuck on, Why in the world would you choose to spend a Saturday morning like this? She could have been at the market, or in bed with Drew, her husband. She has a husband. *Earth to Kate! She has a husband.*

Lauren's voice broke me from my thoughts. "Would you ever date someone like me?"

"Like *you*?" I said the words slowly and deliberately like they had just appeared in the English language for the first time.

"Yes, like *me*," she stressed with her tongue and lips.

I was so transfixed by the sound and the movement of her mouth, that I didn't answer immediately.

"Was I not clear?"

I quickly shook the thoughts from my head as she waited on my answer. "No."

"No? I wasn't clear?"

"No, I wouldn't date someone like you."

"Why?" She seemed surprised, almost caught off guard, which tilted me on my axis.

"I have a strict no dating straight girls policy." I reached into my pocket and pulled out the lining. "Damn it." I snapped my fingers together in mock-disappointment. "I usually keep that policy on me at all times." I winked as she looked at me oddly. "It just gets messy. It's like eating an ice cream sandwich in the dead of summer. It sounds like a good idea, but then the ice cream melts everywhere and the sandwich cookie bits stick to your fingers, and no matter how hard you try, you just can't find a napkin."

"That makes absolutely no sense."

"About as much sense as a lesbian dating a straight girl. This is why I carry that policy on me at all times. It clearly sets out the rules in black and white." I teased again and reached into my other pocket and pulled out the lining. "Damn it. You can never find it when you need it." I stopped my teasing when a hurt look crossed her features. "It's not you. Well, it's totally you, but you're also *really* married. In conclusion, I would never date someone *like you*."

Her eyes widened. "I'm not hitting on you. I'm just asking hypothetically."

I brought my hand over my heart in jest, but I could feel the small crack that had just been created. "You know I have an ego, right? It's a fragile little thing."

She ignored me. "Have you dated bisexual women before?"

"I have."

"But not straight girls…"

"No, straight girls are straight and they date men, not women. Do you need me to give you a lesson on the subject?" I grinned.

"But you're fine with bisexuals?"

"I believe we've already established that. Are you trying to set me up with someone?"

The wheels in my head started to turn, but before they could get anywhere, she said,

"No. Why would you think that?"

"Why do you care so much about who I date? I'm content to play the long game."

"The long game?"

"Good things come to those who wait. We can't all find Prince Charming at age twenty-one." I gave her a knowing look.

"What does that mean?"

I shrugged because I didn't mean anything by it, but the statement hung in the air between us like a weight. Was it my words or my tone that made me sound like a condescending asshole? I honestly couldn't decide, but I knew deep down that it wasn't my intention. "I don't mean anything by it. Truthfully? I never knew he was married and I'm in almost every class with him. He never talks about you…" I said softly because I felt guilty saying it and it wasn't my guilt to have. If Lauren were my wife, I never would have shut up about her and the fact that he said nothing was telling.

"Do you talk about being single?"

"Endlessly!" I laughed at her deflection to try and ease some of the tension. "You and I hardly know one another, and you've brought it up multiple times."

"We know each other."

When she said nothing else, I decided to move our conversation back to safer territory. "I really didn't mean anything by it. Not all of us are that lucky, especially that young," I said gently, not wanting to be disdainful once again. "I'll find her, or she'll find me. I'm in no rush to settle down or get married, no offense."

"How many women have you dated?"

I rolled my eyes and sighed deeply. This subject was starting to become maddening. It always came back to this. Me and women. Women and me. Me and other women was the last thing that I wanted to talk about with Lauren. "Seventeen-hundred-million. You should see the notches on my belt." When her expression turned sour, it was time for me to bring a little bit of levity to the table. "I haven't dated that many women."

"Who was your first girlfriend?"

I brought my hand to my heart and let out a soft sigh. "Sweet, Alex." I meant it. The kind of woman that you marry, but I knew that I never would. "Neither one of us really knew what we were doing at the time. We dated for about six months. Really nice girl."

"What happened?"

"She was more invested than I was. She saw the sunset when she looked at me and I didn't. I knew that I never would. So, I let her go or forced her to let me go."

"You broke her heart." It was more of a statement than an accusation.

"I hope not." But I knew that it was the truth and a part of me still regretted the way that I had treated her.

"Why didn't you just continue to date?"

"I didn't want to waste her time. She had a lot of wonderful qualities. They would have been better spent on someone who was as invested. Do you think it's possible for two people to be as equally enamored, or do you think it's always a little more one-sided?"

"I think it's possible."

"Of course, you do. You've got that with Drew."

She didn't say anything; she just kept scanning the books, helping me when she could have been doing anything else. It was a fact that I kept circling, but I didn't want to overthink it. I tended to read too much into things, to deconstruct and reconstruct what I wanted. I did my best not do that with her, as I didn't have the luxury. I wasn't permitted to stroll with a tune in my mind and conjure up any what-ifs between us. It was impossible since they simply didn't exist in this scenario.

"Do you believe in soul mates?"

"I don't know. What's a soul?" Why were we having these existential conversations here, now, at this ungodly hour, when I was barely caffeinated? I didn't ask this out loud, because I could listen to her ask me a thousand different questions on the most irrelevant and meaningless of subjects.

She didn't say anything for the longest time and then, "A part of you that you can't escape."

"You mean a stalker?" I joked, which earned me a nudge from her foot.

"I'm being serious."

"So am I."

She fixed me with a look like she wasn't going to let it go, like she wanted an answer.

"I like your definition. Something you can't escape." I played the words around in my head. "It makes it seem inevitable and I think that there's something very romantic about that, a destiny perhaps."

"But do you believe it?"

"Yes. I believe that there are those who we are tied too, but at the same time, I believe that we can untie ourselves from them."

"Why would you want to do that?"

"Just because you have a soul mate doesn't mean that it's going to work out or be a healthy relationship. What if your soul mate is an asshole?"

She laughed. "Then they aren't your soul mate."

"All or nothing?"

"Isn't there a beauty in that?"

She was right. There was a beauty in all or nothing, but it wasn't something that I wanted to get into at this moment with her. It wasn't something that I wanted to confess that I pointed my internal compass toward. There were some things she simply didn't need to know. "It's beautiful until your soul mate turns out to be an asshole stalker and then you have to go into the witness protection program."

She kicked me again. "I told you that's not how it works."

"I'm supposed to take your word for it?"

"Yes, I'm the foremost leading expert on soul mates. I've got a Ph.S."

"But of course, you married Prince Charming." I kicked the ball back in her court, but she let it bounce right on by until it came to a stop and she became quiet once again. I let it go and moved onto something a little lighter. "What are you going to do today?"

"This." She got up and changed the order of two of the books on the shelf.

Damn. She was better than me after all. It was the beginning of the end of my job. "As much as I appreciate the help, and I do, get out of here. Find Drew and go and do something fun."

"Can you go five minutes without mentioning him?" Her words were quiet, but still, there was a slight bite to them.

"Yes, I can." I paused for a moment and said, "I can go the rest of this morning without mentioning him." *I can go the rest of my life without mentioning him.*

She didn't say anything, but I couldn't ignore the slight nod of her head as she focused intently on the books in front of her.

We stayed like that all morning, Lauren beside me, not touching, but almost touching as we scanned the spines and she asked me every question that popped into her mind. I answered every single of one them, because what other choice did I have? It felt somewhat inevitable.

CHAPTER NINE

The phone rang when I was busy in the kitchen getting ready for dinner. "Jack, get the phone," I called as I tossed the salad.

She sighed loudly, but she got up from the sofa and picked up the phone. "Hello? Hi, Ms. Dawson! I know... I know... But Mom says that's what I have to call you," she whispered, but it was purposely loud enough for me to hear.

I smiled and shook my head.

Jack walked into the kitchen and held out the phone. "It's Ms. Dawson. She wants to speak to you."

"Ms. Dawson," I said matter-of-factly. I needed to make this as formal and businesslike as possible, no cracks in my armor. I didn't want her light to shine through.

"*Kate*," she said softly and I stopped breathing for an instant as my heart melted just a little. The long pause that accompanied that one word, allowed me to get my bearings as she spoke again. "I'm calling about the sleepover."

I stopped with the dressing. That word from her lips brought me back to our sleepovers. They were everything that I had tried to forget over the years—unhurried fingertips, trembling lips, and the weight of her words as they pressed into my spine. I quickly shook away the thoughts when she spoke again.

"The girls want to have a sleepover." She clarified like she somehow knew that I had taken a trip down memory lane. "Are you okay with this?"

"No, but it doesn't matter what I want," I said quietly and dropped the tongs on top of the salad.

"Do you mind if Abbie stays over on Saturday?"

"It's fine with me if it's fine with you."

"It's fine with me."

I looked over to the clock on the stove. We still had another twenty minutes until dinner was ready. "May I speak with Abbie?"

"Why?"

"Because I'd like to hammer out some of the details with her about the sleepover."

"Shouldn't you and I do that?"

"You won't be sleeping in my house, so no, I don't need to speak to you about the details." I prided myself on my civility, but I also needed to continue to survive in this tiny town with Lauren Dawson. Formal and direct would have to be my touchstones when it came to her.

There was a pause over the line, a sigh, and then the phone was passed to Abbie.

"Hi, Abbie," I said excitedly into the phone, warming my voice a few degrees.

"Hi, Kate."

"I think you're coming to sleepover on Saturday. I'm going to put you on speakerphone so that Jack can hear. We've got important things to discuss. I need you to tell me all of your favorite foods and movies."

I half-listened as Jack and Abbie mindlessly chatted away. My ears strained for any sounds from the other line that didn't involve either of the girls, but I never heard any.

* * *

Jack looked up from her homework. "Mom, I'm going to marry Abbie when I get older."

The words tumbled out like a runaway train.

The thought of being tied to Lauren's family for eternity was more that I could bear at the moment, but Jack didn't need to know any of that. I could feel a headache coming on.

"Okay," I said indifferently. I thought of all the things I'd wanted at Jack's age that had never come to fruition, and I knew that her words were just the young whiskey words of a little girl who was, thankfully, more than a decade away from the taste.

"There's nothing wrong with it!"

The headache arrived. "I know that, baby." Very early on I had taught Jack about the PG-version of the birds and the bees, along with sexuality, the spectrum and a whole host of other age-related topics, and apparently, she was listening at the time.

She pointed at me. "You like girls."

"I like women," I clarified. She might have missed some of the finer points.

"I like girls," she proclaimed loudly, pointing at herself.

I pinched the bridge of my nose to ease some of the tension. I didn't care who Jack was attracted too, who she was interested in, or who she would want to date. But, goddamn it, *not yet*. I was still dealing with the harsh realities that she would rather hang onto her backpack straps than my hands. The thought that she would want to hold someone else's hand, and not mine, was just too much for a Wednesday evening. I hated being a dream crusher. If anything, I was a dream encourager, but not today. "You know what? Why don't you just worry about being a really great friend to Abbie and enjoy being kids? You don't need to worry about who you're going to marry. That's literally forever from now." *If I have anything to say about it.* "If you still feel this way when you're thirty-five, we can talk."

"*Thirty-five!* That's forever."

"Exactly. You don't need to worry about it. Whoever you want to marry when you get older, I'll support it. Even if you never want to get married, I'll support that too."

"How come you never got married?"

It wasn't the first or second time that the question had come up between us. It was a conversation that came up once in a blue moon. I indulged her and we talked about it every time because a part of me worried that she missed the other parent. However, when we got into the ins-and-outs of the discussion, it never appeared to be the case. At the end of the day, Jack was just a romantic at heart. She was always rooting for the kiss at the end of the animated movie and for whatever reason, she couldn't understand why dear old mom didn't have someone with whom to share happily ever after.

"I've already told you multiple times," I offered like I had done so many times in the past.

"You never met the right person." Jack recited the words that had become my mantra during these conversations.

It was a complete and utter lie, but she didn't need to know that at this age or perhaps ever. The older she got, and the more often this conversation came up, I didn't see the need to tell her about my past, for a variety of reasons. I didn't want to teach her about the intricacies of unrequited love and loss. I just hoped that without my explanations, she could avoid the pitfalls altogether. "That's it." I snapped my fingers together. "You need to meet the right person, and sometimes it doesn't happen." I left it at that. I always left it at that.

If I truly subscribed to the fact that all you need is love, then the unrequitedness of it all, especially when I knew the other person did indeed exist was just a little more madness than I wanted to accept or think about. I never wanted Jack to think that she couldn't come and talk to me about anything, especially her sexuality, love, loss, or life. But this was the one subject that I never wanted to discuss with the only person that I was sworn to protect from the dangers of life and the snares of love. I had taken an oath at her adoption ceremony to guide her and I took it as a blood oath. But for some reason, in this instance, I couldn't be her compass and point her down the right path, especially when I didn't have my own sense of direction. My only option was to hand her some provisions, teach her the direction of the stars, and wish her the best of luck. What more did any of us really have?

"Mom, I've met the right person."

"At the tender age of ten."

"Yes!"

My sarcasm was still a little bit lost on her. "Well…" I thought about my next words because I didn't want to break her heart; that would come in enough time. "You hold onto that. Not many people I know can say they knew who they were going to marry at the age of ten. Maybe no one. If it happens, people will say that you had a fated love."

"What's that?"

"That it was meant to be. Written in the stars. The natural order of things…"

"Cool."

"Very cool. Not many people find it and when they do, they usually don't recognize it and they let it pass them by."

"Is that what happened to you?"

A pirate… I shook my head; she had sold herself short. She was smart now, but she would be brilliant in twenty years, curing cancer or world hunger, or seeing past all the bullshit and calling it like it was. Unfortunately, she was just slightly off base in her assessment of me. She had years to fine-tune those skills.

"I'd never let that happen to me. Like I said, if you find it, you hold on for dear life and you never let go. Unfortunately, it takes two people to hold on, not just one."

She picked up her pencil and put her head back down to the math problem that was in front of her. She looked back up at me. "She didn't hold onto you," she said quietly and it was a punch right to the center of my abdomen.

I bit down on my lip, but the mask remained firmly in place. I pointed down to her homework. "The answer is thirty-six."

She was growing up too fast.

A second passed between us and I could tell that she had more questions, but they never came. I was thankful when she scratched out the answer to her math problem, not because I had told her, but because she had double-checked it herself. That night, no more questions came about marriage, Abbie, love, or loss. It was clear she was starting to piece the puzzle together, and one day, when she made sense of it all, I'd at least have to acknowledge the accomplishment, but not tonight.

CHAPTER TEN

Fifteen years earlier

I was being punished for something that I hadn't yet done. Being slapped on the hand before it even came within inches of the cookie jar. That's how I felt with Lauren beside me, her legs stretched out, wearing a perfectly appropriate skirt. It wasn't the two inches above her knees that had me transfixed. Instead, it was the dark gray stockings with the French honeycomb pattern that kissed her skin. It was the closest that I had ever come to understanding the term, "the bee's knees," and it was so fitting.

"What are you doing here, Lauren?" I finally stood, trying to get some distance between us, as I picked up a book from the cart to distract myself from the swarm in my mind.

"What do you mean?"

"It's Friday night." I stated the obvious and gestured to the ghost town that was the library. "It's late. You should be out, or with Drew, or something, anything, but *here*." Not that I didn't love the library, but if I had someone at home waiting to spend time with me, that would have been the only place I'd want to be.

"Drew's at a pickup game with his friends. Can't you be my something?" She gave me a look and it pulled me in one direction. Thankfully, when she stood up from the floor and picked up a book from the cart, it broke the spell.

"I guess." I shrugged. "I don't know if I'd want to follow me and my book trolley around on a Friday night."

"Any plans this weekend?"

"For the first time in a while, I can actually say that I do. What do married people do on the weekends?" I joked, but I secretly wondered.

"Chores, readings, a shift at the coffee shop on Sunday."

"Thrilling," I teased. "I can't wait until I say, 'I do.'"

"What do single people do on the weekends, again?"

"Hopefully get laid. My friend is coming into town." I grinned.

The book that she was holding fell from her hands and landed on the floor with a loud thud.

"A lady friend?" she asked as she completely ignored the book that was helplessly sitting in a heap.

"Well, she's definitely a friend, but not much of a lady." I winked, but the joke was completely lost on her. I reached down to pick up the forgotten book since Lauren seemed to be in no rush to come to its rescue. I smoothed out some of the creased pages before I put it in its proper place. "I'm kidding. Steph's a really nice girl."

"Did you guys ever date?"

"Forever ago, but it wasn't meant to be. We weren't very compatible. It wasn't written in the stars."

"How long did you date?"

I thought about it for a second. "A couple of months. A whirlwind romance. We loved, we lost, we strangely became friends."

"Why's that strange?"

"I've never stayed friends with any of my ex-girlfriends, just Steph."

"Did you love her?"

"Do you mean was I in love with her? No." I shook my head. "She's a good friend."

"So, where will Steph be sleeping when she comes to visit?"

"She'll stay in my bed. It was our one area of compatibility." I winked, but again the joke was lost on her. Tough crowd.

We fell back into a silent rhythm of sorting books and my mind wandered to Steph and my upcoming plans.

"What did you mean that it wasn't written in the stars?"

"Our signs weren't compatible at all. I knew it when we started dating, but I completely ignored it. That's not the kind of thing that you should ignore."

She gave me an odd look like it didn't fit my modus operandi. "You believe in that stuff?"

I shrugged.

"Are we compatible?" she asked after a moment and it felt like the most loaded question that I had ever been asked in my life.

I didn't want to answer but the look in her eyes told me that she wasn't going to let it go. "What's your sign?"

"Cancer."

As soon as she said the word, I couldn't suppress the, "Damn" that escaped my mouth. Unfortunately, she caught it and refused to let it go.

"What?"

"Nothing." I shook my head as I reached for another book.

"Doesn't sound like nothing."

It didn't necessarily fit my MO but it interested me. When I thought about the different women I had dated, I was compatible with some and passionate with others. There was no rhyme or reason to it, but I needed to know why I clicked with some women and not with others. Astrology offered a fun way of sorting it all out.

"Our signs are compatible," I finally offered.

"How compatible?"

"It doesn't matter." I laughed nervously. "I'm the only one that believes in it."

"Tell me."

I waved my hand in the air to dismiss it. "Oh, I don't know... something about karmic debts and reliving love stories of the past." The idea sounded incredibly romantic and I had remembered it to this day.

"Are you feeding me a line?" she teased.

"Is it working?" I was happy that the tension was finally gone from our earlier conversation.

"Maybe." She tilted her head with an adorable smile.

At that moment, I knew that whatever the hell this was, our ballooning friendship was an epic disaster waiting to happen. I had to poke some holes into the friendship balloon before it became completely unmanageable. "I don't need to use lines with women. Just ask Steph."

The sweet smile that was on her face only seconds before, fell just as I had suspected it would. I didn't want to hurt Lauren. It was the last thing I wanted to do, but I didn't want to hurt myself even more. I knew that this was going to hurt me even more. I could feel it in the glances, the almost touches, my thoughts and words, even though there was no place for them to exist.

We shelved a few more books in relative silence and then I turned back to her. "I'm going to close up soon. Thanks for keeping me company."

"I'm going to wait until you're done. Did you drive today?"

"No, I walked."

"I'll give you a ride home."

"You don't need to do that."

"I don't like the thought of you walking this late at night."

"I'm a big girl. I can take care of myself."

"It's not an argument you're going to win."

We drove with the windows down, the radio turned up and a cool breeze swirling throughout the car. We sang badly to a nineties pop song that we both still knew every single word to. When she came upon my street, she parked across from the triplex underneath a streetlight. She cut the engine and the comfortable feeling that was created on the drive over remained with us.

"So, this is where you live?"

"Third floor." I pointed up to the top floor with the little balcony off my one-bedroom apartment.

Neither one of us made any move to leave and the sounds from the night filtered in. It felt too good being here with her and as soon as I was hit by the realization that I was holding onto a feeling with a married woman. It was time to call it a night.

"Thanks for the ride." I offered a smile and reached for the door. Before I could grasp the handle, Lauren threw her arms around my shoulders and pulled me into an awkward half hug.

I didn't push her away when I should have, but I didn't make it easy for her either, as my arms remained at my sides. "What are you doing?" I asked as she pulled me a little closer.

"Getting payment for the car ride." She joked. "You're a terrible hugger."

"Is that what this is? I didn't realize that I would be charged a fare," I said softly into her ear. "Actually, I'm a great hugger. I just didn't know that's what we were doing. Since when do we hug?"

She shrugged in my arms.

"Back up for a second?" I asked, because she was making no move to leave.

She moved away fractionally, and I opened my arms as an invitation. She was in them a second later. It was more than a rookie mistake and I knew it, but I couldn't help myself. Her fragrance, the one that I was desperate to ignore for weeks, invaded my senses. A small hum-sigh escaped her lips and a smile was permanently implanted on mine.

I brought my mouth next to her ear. "See? Great hugger."

She didn't say anything, just sunk into me a little further and it felt perfect.

"Am I paid in full?" I asked after a couple seconds, knowing that we needed to break the hug. I gave one last squeeze and pulled away. When I looked at her, her expression was unreadable, but I knew that a tension that wasn't present in the car moments before had crept between us.

"Kate, can I ask you something?"

"Of course," I said gently trying to soothe the temperament of whatever had joined us in the car.

But no words came out and after a couple of moments she looked away. "Never mind."

"Are you sure? You can ask me anything."

She nodded and looked down at her watch. I knew that our time was up. It was getting late, and if not now, then very soon she would be expected to be home with her husband. I knew that I needed to get out of the car, but I also knew that I felt like unbuckling the strap to her watch, gently removing it from her wrist and pocketing the damn thing so that we weren't constantly in some never-ending countdown.

She broke me from my thoughts. "Have fun with your friend. Come by the shop after class and fill me in on the details."

"I will. Have a good weekend with Drew."

It was the first time I had said something to her that I didn't mean and it burned on my insides. I didn't want her to have a good time with Drew, and I suspected that she really didn't want to know any of the details of my weekend with Stephanie come Monday.

We were both being polite.

We continued to be polite for the next twenty minutes, until I finally forced myself out of her car, up my steps and into my apartment. I closed the door and locked all three locks, to ensure that I would not be tempted to head back down to that car, which continued to idle until I turned on the lights inside my apartment.

Damn it.

CHAPTER ELEVEN

The day had finally arrived for the larger-than-life sleepover. It was impossible not to take note of the most important event that was happening in Jack's life, as I heard about it every single day in the lead up to Saturday. When the knock came on the door, Jack raced to the front of the house and I called out, "Look before you open the door."

"*I know*," she sassed quietly. "It's Abbie and Ms. Dawson," she yelled and opened the door quickly. Jack threw her arms around Abbie's neck and gave her a quick hug. "We're going to have the best time." She took the bag from Abbie's hand.

I smiled at her chivalry, at least she picked up some of the finer points from me.

"Let's put this in my room," Jack said to Abbie.

While the exchange between the girls unraveled, Lauren stood quietly off to the side, obviously feeling a little out of place and I couldn't blame her after our few brief interactions.

"Do you want to come in for a second?" I asked as she hovered near the threshold, her hands rested in her back pockets. I couldn't tell if she was watching Abbie walk away or staring into the rest of my home.

"Sure." She walked past me into the living room. She studied the small space, but her gaze quickly turned to the record player sitting under the windowsill. "You still have it," she said surprised. She walked over to the record player and lifted the arm gently but she didn't place the needle down on the record. I waited for it to happen, just like she had done a number of times in the past. I held my breath, but she placed the needle back in the cradle and turned to face me.

I exhaled. "Nope. Dad's died. I know it looks the same, but it's a newer model. Who knew they would come back in style?"

Lauren looked like she had transported herself away from the moment, and I was certain that I knew where she was. I cleared my throat to get her attention. When she finally looked back at me, there was a look in her eyes that I recognized. She opened her mouth to speak and I could practically see the words on the tip of her tongue, but I pushed away the desire to acknowledge whatever memory she was stuck on and deflected as only I could. "Anything crazy that I should know before we embark on the sleepover?"

She closed her mouth, shook her head fractionally and pursed her lips. The look was gone and replaced with a slight irritation, which to me, came across as completely endearing. "You didn't hammer out those details with Abbie?" she said with a pointed tone.

"All she wanted to talk about was pizza and unicorn movies. I tuned out after a while. Jack listened *very* carefully, though, so if something comes up on either one of those two subjects in the next few hours, I'm going to defer to Jack."

Lauren pulled a unicorn night-light from her bag and held it out in her hand. "She has a hard time sleeping without a night-light."

"She'll be fine." I offered a reassuring smile as I reached for the light. "I told the strippers to come after I get the girls into bed." I winked.

"You hate strippers."

"Says who?" I declared loudly and put my hand to my chest, the horn of the unicorn making its presence known as it jabbed into my breastbone. "You?"

"You like leaving those sorts of things to your imagination."

"You act like you know me."

"Don't I?"

"No." I had to swallow back the sadness that had started to creep into my voice. "I was a stupid kid back then. What the hell did I know? I'm older now and hopefully a little wiser. I don't want to leave anything else to my imagination. Bring on the strippers."

A small vein throbbed in her neck and she turned back to the record player.

I needed to find a way to end the conversation, get her out of the living room and out of my house, as my insufferable imagination was starting to take its own trip down memory lane. "Anything else?" I asked.

"She's not really good at sleepovers."

"That makes two of us. If she tries to sneak out in the middle of the night, Jack will find her." I could see the look of apprehension in her eyes and I eased my playfulness. "We'll be fine, I promise. If *anything* comes up, if she wants to leave, I'll bring her home right away."

"Kate," she started and I didn't know if it was a statement or a question. "We don't have to hate each other." Definitely a statement.

I studied her. Arms folded tightly across her chest, shoulders that looked like steel couldn't penetrate them, and a pair of green eyes that tried to mask a vulnerability that she never could hide from me. I felt overwhelmed at that moment because my actions were the cause of that helplessness. "Lauren, I don't hate you," I said softly. I could never hate her, even if the pain that existed between us was a thousand times greater.

"You don't like me."

I sighed when I realized that it was going to take more than a few hollow words to put an end to this conversation. "That's not true. The truth is that I don't feel anything toward you anymore." I took a deep shameful breath. What was the harm in a little white lie at this point in time? "It took a long time for me to get there, but I did. That's where I have to stay."

That last part was especially true and I couldn't deviate from that truth for even a second. I had rebuilt my life without her. How someone who had only been present for less than a year could completely undo every aspect of me, was something that still baffled me to this day. I had spent more sleepless, half-sober nights pondering that reality. After the first couple of years, I just accepted it as some sort of fate for a crime that I had committed in another life. It must have been horrendous, and I must have gotten off on a technicality at trial. And this life, this burden, was my punishment.

"I'm sorry." Her words broke me from my thoughts.

I shook my head. "You don't need to apologize." I smiled and tried to make it come across as genuine, but it felt slightly off-center. "You can come and pick up Abbie after breakfast if you want."

She nodded and walked toward the bottom of the stairs. "Abbie, I'm leaving," she called.

"Bye," Abbie shouted, not making any move to leave Jack's room.

Lauren held out her hands, palm up, as she looked up the stairs.

I felt bad for her. It was backpack straps all over again, but of course, I couldn't let the moment go. "Can you blame her? I mean… Jack is *my* daughter. We're irresistible." I wiggled my eyebrows and then scrutinized her closely. "Except for you." I shrugged. "It must have skipped a generation. Just my luck." I snapped my fingers in mock-disappointment.

Lauren gave me a look which was either a mixture of flipping me off or preparing herself to get into a full-blown argument. Thankfully, she moved to the front door. "Good night, Kate."

After she closed the door, I wanted to sink into the floor with my thoughts for the better part of a week, but I had a sleepover to get through.

CHAPTER TWELVE

Fifteen years earlier

When I walked into my first women's literature class the Monday after the break, I did a double take, because seated third row from the front was Lauren.

"Kate," she called and waved me over.

I stood at the front of the class dumbfounded and popped my head back outside of the door to look at the number to make sure that I had the right room. I did. Perhaps, she was in the wrong class. "What are you doing here?" I looked down and noticed that she carried the same copy of *The Bell Jar* that was tucked away in my bag.

"When you told me about the course, I looked into it, and it seemed like a fun class. I saved you a seat." She pulled out the chair immediately next to her. "I've already read a lot on the reading list; you're going to really enjoy this class."

"Why did you take it then?"

She shrugged and then I shrugged internally because denial was a very lovely river this time of year. It was time for one of us to fess up. "The reading list looks great, but to be honest I have ulterior motives. I was hoping to scope out my options."

"Options?"

I looked around at the other seats and it was ninety-nine-point-nine percent women. I gestured to the class with my eyes and wiggled my eyebrows. There was only one young man, who obviously had the same idea as me.

"Oh, right. Good thing I'm here. I can help you find someone. I could be your wingman, wing-woman, whatever."

"You will?" I asked surprised. All of our shared moments flashed before my eyes. Had I read everything wrong? It's not like I had that many straight female friends. Maybe this was how they all acted.

"Definitely, I have great taste."

Even though there was a little twinge of disappointment that I had interpreted the situation incorrectly, I felt instant relief. We'd be partners in crime. "This is going to be so much fun."

She quickly looked away. "*So* fun."

Once class began and the professor was reviewing the syllabus for the semester, I picked up Lauren's pen and scribbled on her paper, *Right-hand side of the room, 4th row, 2nd seat.*

I pushed the paper toward her. She read it carefully and then discreetly looked over to the right side of the room. After ten seconds she scribbled back, *You can do better…*

I smiled; this was going to be fun.

CHAPTER THIRTEEN

I scrolled through the online catalog as I tried to find the missing links and made a mental list of the new titles that we would need for the new semester. As I was semi-engrossed in my task, I spotted a woman walk past my desk, stop dead in her tracks, and call out a bit too loudly for the library, "Kate?"

I looked up from the computer and found a familiar pair of brown eyes that I hadn't seen in at least a year. "Patricia." I double-checked my surroundings. I was still in the library. The last time I had seen her was on the other side of a boardroom table. We had worked together briefly when I still lived in the city, but our paths only crossed a handful of times. We had shared a few coffees, but due to work schedules, it never went any further than that.

She gave me a double-take. "What are you doing here?"

"Career change." I smiled warmly. "I could ask you the same thing."

She handed me a faculty card with the college logo on it. I took it and ran it through the scanner attached to my computer. "You're teaching law here?"

She brushed her hair back behind her ear and gave me a lopsided grin. "I don't know if *teaching* would be the right word. I'm giving a seminar on the day-to-day aspects of the law. I talk and answer most of my own questions." She looked down at my desk. "I didn't know that you left private practice. This is quite the career change."

"It's not that big of a stretch. I was a librarian before I went into law. I needed a change or a change back…" I rambled and thankfully she let the subject drop.

"How's Jack?"

"She's good, thanks."

"I hate to cut this short, but I've got to get to my class. Can we catch up sometime?"

"I'd like that."

* * *

Two weeks after the sleepover, Jack cornered me in the kitchen over breakfast one morning. I was knee-deep into a lukewarm cup of instant coffee and caught in a daydream when she put down her spoon and cleared her throat. "May I sleep over at Abbie's?" she asked with quiet confidence.

I was especially pleased when she used the word *may*. She rarely asked me for anything and when she did, I almost always said yes, but under the current circumstances, all I wanted to say was no.

"You just had a sleepover."

"Yes, but it was here. We want to have one at Abbie's."

"I don't know…" I started and her face fell. "Let me think about it, okay?" I felt almost guilty by denying her something that in all likelihood I would concede in the end.

My hesitation caught her off guard, but she left it alone. "Okay, Mom." She released a soft sigh and I felt like a monster.

"I'm not saying no. Just let me think about it." I reached over and squeezed her hand.

She got up from the table, put her dish in the sink and headed upstairs. I sat there, coffee now cold, shaking my head slowly. I knew that denying a friendship for my daughter because

I couldn't deal with the pain from my past was a terrible reason to do so. I sat for a few minutes and then picked up the phone and sighed loudly. I dialed Lauren's number and she answered on the second ring.

"Yes, Kate?" a short and clipped greeting, no doubt as a result of our last exchange and my last jab.

"May I speak to Abbie?" I asked as pleasantly as possible.

"Is this about the sleepover that I've been hearing about all day?"

"So, this is already a forgone conclusion, isn't it? You and I are the only ones standing in the way of the fated sleepover."

"You're the only one standing in the way." It didn't feel like she was talking about the sleepover at all.

"May I please speak to Abbie?" I asked again because I didn't want to go anywhere near the glacier that was Lauren's current tone.

"No, you can't speak to Abbie. You can speak to me."

I swallowed hard but made damn sure that no sound escaped. She wasn't going to make this easy for me. Why should she? I hadn't made it easy for her and I had no intention to do so going forward. "I'd rather hammer out the details with your daughter."

"It's my house. You can hammer them out with me."

I had heard that voice before, at least once, and I knew better than to argue. I sighed dramatically into the phone. "Can Jack sleepover at your house?"

"Yes."

"This Saturday?"

"Yes."

"Six?"

"Five, we eat early."

"Fine."

"Fine."

"That was some fun hammering. Nice talking to you, Lauren. See you on Saturday." I hung up and drained the bitter contents in one swallow. "You're doing this for Jack," I said over and over. Be the better person, I encouraged the little devil sitting on my left shoulder, but we both knew better who would win in the end.

CHAPTER FOURTEEN

Fifteen years earlier

Our professor walked around the room, talking to herself more than anyone else about our next assignment. I only tuned in when the two worst words in the English language passed her lips consecutively and evaporated into the classroom.

Group work.

A signup sheet was placed in front of me and I eyed it wearily. I hated group work. I hated relying on anyone other than me, myself, and I.

Lauren leaned in as my pen hovered over the paper. "We're partners, right?" she asked but it really wasn't a question as the distinct tone in her voice told me that it was a statement, which she was asking me to confirm.

I was perfectly fine with the arrangement. I got to work with the most beautiful girl in the class who was also the most brilliant. If anything, it seemed like a monumental victory on my part. If this was group work, I could definitely get on board with it. "Of course." I shrugged like it was the most obvious answer. After all, it wasn't like she was going to let me work with *right-hand side of the room, fourth row, second seat,* not in this life or the next.

"Do you want to get together tonight to work out the logistics?"

"Sure, I have a short shift at the library. Where do you want to work on it?" I left the ball in her court and secretly hoped that she would pick any other location than her apartment.

"Can I meet you at your place?"

That surprised me as I thought for sure that she would opt for the library. I would have preferred neutral territory, but I reminded myself that she was straight, married, and in no way interested in me.

"Okay, eight? Do you need me to write down the address or do you remember?"

"I remember."

When I opened the door later that evening, Lauren stood in the hallway with her book bag in one hand and a bottle of something in the other.

"You found it." I smiled as I moved past the threshold to let her pass. When she did, she handed me a bottle of whiskey. Not my brand, but something even better. "What's this for?"

"For hosting tonight," she said as she took in my apartment.

It wasn't much, but I adored the old fireplace and the hardwood floors that were beyond repair. Floors that I had to be mindful of when I cleaned, out of fear that I would dislodge a hundred-year-old floorboard and never get it back into place.

"I thought you had a one bedroom?" Her gaze was fixed on my bed at the far end of the living room, with a thick curtain, tied back, separating it from the rest of the space.

A small lump formed in the back of my throat. "I do, but it's too small to be considered a bedroom. It's really just a storage space now. I close the curtains at night," I blurted and immediately cursed myself. "Are you ready to get started on the project? One of us can work on the summary and one of us can prepare the questions. I don't really care which I do. I don't even think we'll need to spend that much time on it tonight as long as we both know our roles…"

She finally looked at me and when she did, I realized that I hadn't asked for her coat, her bag, or offered to get her something to drink. All the common and polite pleasantries that I would have offered to even my most mortal enemies, fell by the wayside at the mere sight of Lauren transfixed on a bed in the living room.

"Are you nervous?" she asked.

"Nervous? *Me*?" I reached for her bag. "Let me take your things. Would you like something to drink?"

She confidently smiled. "You're doing it again." She pointed at me like she had just put her finger on the button, but at that moment, it felt like she was pushing all of mine.

"What?"

"You're nervous."

"No." I lied. "I just realized that I was rude when you first came in and I'm trying to fix it."

She considered me thoughtfully for a second and then wandered around my apartment, in no hurry to get to a group project that only one of us seemed to care about. I watched her for a moment and then put her things off to the side and reached for my own bag.

We had the books open for thirty minutes when she looked up from her work and announced that she wanted to take a break. I wanted to argue but other than figuring out our roles, there wasn't much else to do for the evening. I got up, thinking some soft jazz would be perfect for the break, but once the record started to spin I realized my error. I wasn't trying to create a mood, but it happened naturally. When I turned back to Lauren, her forearm was bathed in the soft glow of the reading lamp and it took everything in me not to become permanently fixated on that spot. I shook my head and poured myself a splash of whiskey. "Do you want anything to drink?"

"Can I try a sip of your whiskey?"

I handed her my glass, and her fingers brushed against mine.

"Well?" I could tell that she didn't care for it.

"It's different."

I was surprised when she took another sip. "Do you want a glass?"

"No, I'll just sip from yours if I want any."

I sat down beside her and put the glass between us and focused on the music as it filled the room.

"How long have you had the record player?"

"It belonged to my father."

She reached for the glass and took another tentative sip.

"Next time, I'll get you your own glass."

"I won't want it then." She closed her eyes. "What kind of women do you like to date?"

I chuckled. "Are we on that again? Are you trying to set me up with one of your friends?"

"No, why?"

"Why do you care so much? Am I the first gay person you've ever met?"

"Of course not."

"Sometimes you act like it. I date women that are available. Why does it always come back to this question with you?"

"You're very quiet. If I don't ask you questions, you don't say anything."

It was the truth. I preferred to exist in the silent moments. "What is there to say with this music on?" The low dizzying sound of the trumpet lingered. I pointed to the record player. "The music is so much more interesting. What could you possibly want to know about me with this music on?"

"Everything."

I moved the glass toward my lips, but she stole it from my hand and took another sip.

"I'm tired of talking about me. Why don't we talk about you?"

"What do you want to know?"

Everything, I thought but didn't say. "How did you meet Drew?" I asked, because even though I really didn't want to know, I was curious.

"Our parents were friends for years, and by extension we became friends as well."

"That's nice, right? You got to marry your best friend."

"I wouldn't say he's my best friend..."

"Bosom buddy?"

She rolled her eyes.

"If I get married, I hope she's my best friend."

"Why?"

"Because I'm going to spend the rest of my life with her. A best friend… You want to be around that person all the time. You can't wait for them to wake up to see their smile, hear their voice. They know you inside and out. They know how to make you laugh and they go out of their way to do it. Morning coffee will be all the sweeter. Even the mundane… And when it gets tough, you tough it out together."

"Did you know that another word for best friend is soul mate?" But she didn't let me answer. "I was right."

"About what?"

"You do believe in soul mates."

It was my turn to roll my eyes. "I believe in best friends. Best friends are never stalkers." I winked.

"I like that…"

"What?"

"The idea of ending up with your soul mate."

"Best friend," I corrected her.

"Best friend," she said thoughtfully. No more words came. She continued to sip from my glass of whiskey as the music played softly in the background. Neither one of us touched the fact that even though she was married, she was neither with her best friend or her soul mate.

CHAPTER FIFTEEN

I gave a sour look at the white picket fence as we walked up Lauren's driveway. Jack raced up the stairs and waited for me as I took my time, surveying the green two-story craftsman. With the impatience of my daughter practically seeping through the wooden planks of the front porch, I finally edged toward the door and knocked three times. It only took seconds for it to open, and when it did, Abbie stood with a huge smile on her face. Is that how I looked the first time Lauren came to my house? I hoped not; I would have given away all my secrets that very first night.

"Jack," Abbie cried excitedly. "I never thought you'd arrive."

"I had to finish my chores." Jack looked annoyed at me, with her backpack slung over her shoulder, waiting to be invited in.

"They weren't going to do themselves." I looked down at her with a knowing look and then took a glance over Abbie's head. I could see a comfortable and casual looking Lauren walking down the hallway.

"Come in," she said as she pushed the door further open and guided Jack through the doorway.

I took note of the messy assortment of shoes and bags as Jack carefully undid hers and placed them on the mat by the front door. The girls chatted about the impending variety of excitement and thrills about to occur, and I could barely keep up.

"Here's my cell." I handed over a small sticky note to Lauren who held it in her palm and looked at it curiously. "Just in case you try and reach me and I'm not at the house."

"Mom has a date tonight." Jack spoke up and I shrunk a little.

"You have a date?" Lauren asked.

"Boys are gross." Abbie scrunched up her face and I had to stop myself from giving her a high five.

"I wholeheartedly agree. Boys are gross." I winked and she nodded.

"My mom doesn't date boys. She dates girls," Jack said to Abbie.

"I date women."

"She's going out with Patricia," Jack said to Lauren and I cringed internally.

I reached down and slowly patted my daughter's head, once, twice, three times nice. "You don't have to tell everyone everything," I said gently.

Jack looked up at me. "It's a secret?"

"Of course not. I doubt anyone here cares to know."

Jack held up her hands in confusion.

"It's alright, kiddo." I gave her shoulder a squeeze.

"My mom dates boys," Abbie said to Jack like she was clarifying her favorite flavor of ice cream. *Vanilla*, how trite.

"I've dated girls before," Lauren said quietly to no one in particular, but my ears perked up and I just barely managed to keep my eyes in their sockets.

"You have?" Abbie asked as she looked up at Lauren, her own eyes widening to the size of dinner plates with each passing moment.

"Before your father," Lauren said.

It was a lie, but what else was she going to say? I was blown away that she even acknowledged her bisexuality to Abbie.

I said nothing. There was nothing for me to say. I bent down and hugged Jack. "Have a good time. Please mind your manners because I will be asking Ms. Dawson for a report." I gently tilted her chin until her gaze held mine. "If it's a bad report this will be the final sleepover. Are we clear?"

"Yes," Jack answered quickly and provided me with a salute.

"Have fun." I kissed her temple.

A split-second later, the pair raced up the stairs and Lauren and I stood awkwardly in the entrance. I pushed my hands into my pockets as I was terrified that they would flail helplessly if I didn't. "I don't have any night-lights for you."

"*Patricia?*" she asked like she had been rolling around the name in her mind, making all of the connections. "The new professor?"

"That's the one."

"She's cute," Lauren said but it didn't sound sincere.

"She is. Is it too early to try and convince her to join the book club?" I asked but didn't wait for her response. "It's always such a delicate balance—" I stopped mid-sentence when her look turned into an icy glare. I swallowed. "Too soon?" I asked like the asshole that I was and would always be. "Sorry," I said quietly, when it was obvious that I had struck a very delicate nerve. "I'll pick Jack up at nine?"

"She can stay longer than that."

"That's okay. It's Sunday. I'm sure you've got things you want to get done before the week starts."

"Have fun tonight. Don't do anything I wouldn't do…" She trailed off and I was left with a thousand different images that I didn't want.

A retort sat on the edge of my lips begging to come out, but this wasn't about me or Lauren, or digging up the past, so I refrained.

"Have a good night. If Jack needs anything, call and I'll come right away."

CHAPTER SIXTEEN

Fifteen years earlier

Another study night in the books. Not that either one of us did much studying when she came over to my place. Studying just seemed like a flimsy excuse to spend time together. Instead of organizing her notes, she sorted my collection of records as she sipped from my whiskey glass. I laid on the floor as I read aloud from our current novel of the week, not every syllable, but the words and phrases that moved me. She'd nod or hum in approval and sometimes she would wrap her lips, teeth, and tongue around a particular meaty word until she chewed the meaning right out of it.

It was a chilly start to the winter season, all lion and no lamb, but the boiler in my apartment was almost always reliable. Lauren had just put on one of my favorite Billie Holiday records.

"Listen to this…" I slightly altered my voice.

"Do you want to dance?" Lauren's words floated over the music.

My eyes shot up from the book. She faced the window with her hand hovering over the record player and the only thing that I could really notice was how rigid her body appeared as she waited on my answer. I carefully closed the book and put it off to the side. As the time ticked by and the record spun, she said, "Don't tell me you don't know how to dance. I know better."

"I can dance." *Not well.*

She adjusted the needle and the first few notes of "I'll Be Seeing You" started to play. Had I mentioned that to her before? I couldn't remember, but I wanted to imagine that I had. She finally turned to me. "Well?" She took a step toward me and held out her hand.

"I've never danced with a straight woman before." I don't know why I said that, but my words didn't seem to faze her. I considered her hand for a second longer than I should have, studying the palm, and I wondered how soft it would feel in mine.

"I'm sure it's the same as dancing with one of your girlfriends."

"I doubt that."

"Why?"

"I'm usually trying to make a move when I'm dancing."

"You'd never make a move on me..." The words scattered dangerously between us.

"No, I wouldn't." I considered her hand for another moment and then took it.

As Lauren and I danced, I became engrossed in the window, illuminated by a single streetlight. Heavy snow that had been falling for hours hadn't eased and had started to blanket Renfrew. It was a tranquility that gave a brief reprieve to the uncontrollable storm brewing within me. A thousand thoughts swirled in my mind like snowflakes, no two the same. I couldn't grasp one long enough to give it a second thought before it dissolved completely. I blinked and the light pulled me back to my apartment. A chill crept into my sock-covered feet, and a dull pain shot into my fifth metatarsal, a nagging reminder of an old fracture that never properly healed and left me hobbling around on hundred-year-old floorboards. As Lauren stared at me, I felt as stripped as those old floorboards.

"It's getting late," I whispered, not after the first song or the second, but when we were nearing the end of the record. It was the last thing I wanted to say, but I didn't trust many other words. I just wanted to keep shuffling badly along to a rhythm that I didn't really understand. Thankfully at that moment I didn't need too. I was too focused on a heartbeat that wasn't my own.

"I didn't notice," she replied. Her feet moved with mine but had a grace that I would never possess.

"Your car is probably buried under ten feet of snow." I motioned to the window with my head, but her gaze never left mine.

"Can I stay the night?"

The sound of the record needle being wrenched across the vinyl must have transpired in some alternative dimension because it continued to spin. All of the snowflakes that were fluttering in my mind, whirled until they formed one distinct word, *No!*

"Ummm…" I hesitated and her feet continued to guide mine. "The sofa really isn't that comfortable."

"Can't we share the bed?"

The snow globe that was my mind instantly became a squall and formed into an angry snowman who held up a little sign with the words, *Absolutely Fucking Not!* He did have a good point.

"Ummm…" I mumbled. *Regretfully we cannot share my bed this evening because I'll never be able to think of anything else.*

"Are you going to kick me out, Kate?" she asked playfully, still lost in the music.

I could barely keep up. Was I going to kick her out in the middle of a snowstorm?

"No," I said, resigned. *Damn it.*

The snowman flipped me the middle finger, threw the sign to the ground and plodded away.

"I think I have an extra toothbrush and some pajamas."

I let Lauren get into bed first while I went through my nightly routine. Just before I closed the bathroom door, I overheard the beginning lines of her conversation with Drew about how the roads were too bad to come home and that she was spending the night. I leaned my head back against the bathroom door and closed my eyes. I exhaled and lightly banged the base of my skull against the wood. What the hell was happening? I pushed myself off the door and went to the sink and applied a generous amount of toothpaste to my toothbrush. I desperately tried to avoid the mirror as I brushed at a snail's pace, making sure that I had circled every last tooth. I didn't want to see my reflection or the grin that I knew would sneak out if given the opportunity.

When I had taken up a disproportionate amount of time in the bathroom, I returned to the living room. The light was already shut off and Lauren was just a silhouette facing the window. I eased into bed, desperate not to wake her and laid perfectly still on my back. As soon as I settled, she rolled over to face me. "It's freezing in here." She shuffled closer toward me, a micro-millimeter, but a micro-millimeter nonetheless.

"I know. I'm sorry. It will warm up in a bit. Don't you just love hundred-year-old houses?" I faced her and in the process moved back an inch.

After a moment, Lauren's feet tangled with mine.

"Whoa." I backed away, but she found them again.

"Your feet are like ice," she said, as she rubbed her feet against mine.

"What are you doing?"

"Trying to warm you up."

"I'm warm."

"Liar." She continued to rub my feet. "I can't fall asleep unless I do this."

"Play footsies?"

"It's a comfort thing," she said simply as she continued.

Her habit relaxed me. I was moments away from sleep, which I never thought possible with her resting beside me.

"Are you comfortable?" I asked.

"Yes." She finally stopped moving her feet, but they remained tangled with mine as her breathing became shallow. "I'm glad that I'm here, Kate."

"Me too," I whispered as I started to drift off.
What the hell did that snowman know anyway?

The next morning after Lauren had left, I eyed the T-shirt that she had folded up neatly and left at the end of my bed. Even though I told myself repeatedly that I wasn't going to do it, I picked it up and brought it to my nose. My eyes fluttered closed and I slowly inhaled until I swallowed her scent. I shook my head and a sigh escaped my lips. "This is going to kill you…" My words bounced off every surface in the room but they wouldn't penetrate into anything, including me, so that I would listen. It was a fair-weather warning, which I would ignore, circle back to one day and say… *I told you so.* I inhaled the shirt again and searched my brain. "Lavender…" But there was something else and I couldn't place it.

CHAPTER SEVENTEEN

The next morning, dressed exactly as I had been the afternoon before, I waited on Lauren's front porch. I bounced my knee as I counted down the minutes on my watch. Ten to nine was far too early to knock. I played the events of the previous evening in my mind and continued to bounce my knee. The date with Patricia, if you could call it that, had gone fine. Two friends catching up and enjoying each other's company. But when I left her house, all I could think about was Lauren. The thoughts remained with me until the early morning hours and before I knew it, I was on the verge of being late to pick up Jack.

When I knocked promptly at nine, Lauren answered in sweatpants, a wrinkled jersey, and a messy bun. The combination made me weak in the knees. I mentally inserted a steel rod into my spine and straightened my shoulders. This needed to be quick and painless, or less pain than I was experiencing by her current appearance.

"Good morning." I caught my smile. "Is Jack ready?"

Lauren looked at me for a long moment as she held the door open. She wasn't a morning person and that obviously hadn't changed in all this time. "Isn't that what you wore yesterday?" she asked as she studied my wrinkled button up.

We were both half wrinkled but she didn't appear to find mine endearing. I did my best to ignore it, so I deflected. "How was Jack?"

"Perfect."

I nodded. "Good."

"Do you want to come inside?"

I hesitated. The outdoors was infinitely safer, but I was never safe when it came to Lauren. I stepped inside and she closed the door behind me. It was a peaceful Sunday morning and if I was at home, I would have been in bed, sipping my second cup of coffee.

"She's very well behaved. You don't need to be so hard on her." Lauren's voice broke me from my thoughts.

The rod that I had inserted into my spine only a few moments before became rigid. I looked down at my watch. "I wasn't expecting parenting advice this early in the morning. Thank you for your advice, Lauren. I'll file it under mind your damn business. Was that rude?" I gave an insincere smile. "Mind your damn business, *please*. There we go. So, glad that I could start my day like this."

She ignored my over-the-top rudeness with a shake of her head and I silently reprimanded myself. This was not going at all as I had planned. I didn't mean to come across as a complete jerk, but it felt like all of my words had an edge and bite to them when it came her. Too much time had passed and my once soft edges had become razor-sharp.

"Looks like you've already got a good start to your day." She pointed at my clothes and I kept my rude comments to myself.

"Jack never sleeps this late." I tapped my watch and looked toward the staircase.

"I was going to give them a few more minutes. Good date last night?"

"It was nice," I said quickly, wanting to discuss any other topic on the face of the planet.

"Must have been more than nice…"

It was obvious that she wanted me to fill in whatever blanks she had conjured up in her head as she continued to push the subject. I turned to her. "Do you really want the details?" I warned, even though there were none to give her.

"No." The word slipped quietly between her lips and she crossed her arms.

I gave a fake smile. "Then stop asking about it. I'm not up for twenty questions this morning, especially when we both know the answer is going to be a Crock-Pot." I looked toward the staircase. I had half a mind to go back outside and wait on the porch.

"Are you going to see her again?"

It was the last straw. First, unwelcome parenting advice and now questions to answers that she knew damn well she didn't want. I took a quick step toward her and she backed up, startled by my sudden movements. It was college all over again with her insistent questions about my dating history. I knew how this played out and I didn't need a do-over. Our gazes locked, but my mouth was already off running. "We had dinner at her place. Pasta with this delicious red sauce that her grandmother made when she was younger and red wine. It was a long week for her, so I told her, 'let's just be laid-back.'"

"Kate—"

I took another step, but she held her ground. I shook my head. "I ended up doing most of the cooking. I put on some music. We ate, talked, caught up. The next thing I know she's laughing at some stupid joke of mine. You know, the one about the hippopotamus."

As the corners of her lips curved into a slight smile, I could tell that she had remembered it, but I didn't give her more than a second to linger. "Her hand is on my thigh. She leans forward and her lips brush right here." I pointed to the space between my cheek and lips, which was just a fraction from Lauren's. "She doesn't pull away. She just stays there, lingering. She's so close." I closed my eyes and inhaled for emphasis.

"Kate—"

"She smells so good. Her body is on fire and I haven't even touched her yet." When I opened my eyes, Lauren's were a kaleidoscope of emotions, so of course, I continued to push. "My head is swimming. It's her, the wine, and it's so easy to turn my head and capture her lips…" I leaned forward until my mouth was inches from Lauren's ear. "What else do you want to know? Do you want to know what it felt like when I was inside her? She was definitely warmer than a Crock-Pot."

I welcomed the shove that sent me backward. Hell, I deserved a slap. I moved back into her personal space, not to be menacing, but to make my point crystal clear. Again she held her ground. "Keep prodding. Keep pushing. You better stay away from my cage, Lauren," I warned, but there was no threat behind it. "You don't know the first thing about me anymore. There are a lot more triggers now than there used to be."

"Mom!" Jack yelled in excitement and I immediately backed away from Lauren, almost stumbling in the process. "You're early. We haven't eaten breakfast yet."

I struggled to get my bearings. It felt like there was a pressure on my chest that I couldn't remove. I needed to get out of that house, away from the problem and the past.

"I'm taking you out for breakfast. We'll get pancakes," I said quickly to the girls, still dressed in their pajamas.

"Abbie has to come. You promised we could have breakfast together."

"Abbie can come too," I offered quietly. It was completely out of place. It wasn't my call as to what Abbie did or didn't do. I turned to Lauren to offer an apology, but she wouldn't look in my direction.

"Mom?" Abbie turned to Lauren, who quickly nodded.

When Lauren finally looked at me, her features were a grab bag of emotions. I could see hurt, anger, and something else that looked like jealousy, so of course, I continued to push her. "What about you? Are you *coming* for breakfast?"

"No," she whispered.

"I didn't think so. I'll have her back in an hour. I'll be in the car, girls. First one out gets something with chocolate for breakfast."

I practically ran out of the house and down the front steps. I wanted to dropkick the white picket fence as I passed it. I opened my car door, climbed in and slammed it shut as hard as I could. I felt like an absolute asshole and there was nothing that I could do to change what I had just done.

When I pulled back into Lauren's driveway just under an hour later, I told Jack to stay in the car as I walked Abbie back up the stairs and knocked. Lauren opened the door and Abbie went inside. Before she could close the door in my face, I quickly blurted, "I'm sorry." I held up my hands, palms up.

She opened the door a little further and leaned in the doorway with her arms across her chest.

"I'm sorry..." I said again. "I don't know how to be the bigger person. I didn't then and I'm struggling with it now. I was completely out of line earlier."

"I shouldn't have asked," she finally said. "It's none of my business."

"No, it's not and if you would have just minded your business in college, we probably wouldn't be standing here today, but I didn't need to do that. I never thought when I moved back to Renfrew that you would still be here. It never once occurred to me. I thought you'd be off traveling the world or writing in some exotic location."

"Here I am." Her arms tightened across her chest.

"Here you are," I breathed. "What happened today, won't happen again. I sincerely apologize."

"Let's just forget about it."

She extended her hand and I almost took a step back. Four thousand, three hundred, and eighty days without any physical contact and her hand remained suspended in the air. My manners propelled me forward and I grasped it firmly in mine. We went through the motions, pumping our hands up and down, and I felt completely undone. Her hands were warm and soft, as they had been and always would be. Some things about people were innate and unalterable; Lauren was warm and soft. She was warm and soft with me, even when she didn't have to be.

I headed back to the car, but then turned before she closed the door. "I didn't sleep with Patricia last night. I didn't even kiss her."

Lauren looked at me for a long moment. "Why not?"

I shrugged because I couldn't admit to her that I was stupidly starting to fall for her all over again. "I just didn't."

"But it was a date," she clarified.

"Yeah." I sighed. "It was a date."

CHAPTER EIGHTEEN

Fifteen years earlier

"Did you do the readings for the test?" Lauren asked as she collapsed into the seat next to mine, clearly exhausted. She'd obviously had a long night, but I didn't want to think about any of the reasons why.

"I studied all night. I have to keep up with you, don't I?"

"Can I see your notes?" she asked, but I knew she didn't need them. She never had to study. She just knew the answers. I was in a constant state of awe of the words that she would string together in class when she was called upon to answer a question. She was the real deal and I was just an imposter trying to get by. We would both read the same passage and her interpretation had the elegance and depth of an abstract painting. Her intelligence combined with a fierce wit made me appreciate her in ways that I knew I shouldn't.

"You don't need them." I waved my hands over my notes. "I even had to Google a French word. If you want a free pass to look at these babies, it's going to cost you."

"What word?" Her head was slightly tilted, half-asleep and completely adorable.

"Hmmm?" I asked in a daze as some hair fell across her face.

"The French word," she clarified as she reached for my notes and I didn't do anything to put up a fight.

"*Inoubliable.*" I said it with the best French accent that I could muster, but I butchered it and laughed at my own mispronunciation.

"It means unforgettable or never to be forgotten." She said it like it was on the tip of her tongue the entire time.

I never wrote down the translation in my notes. It's not like I was going to forget never to be forgotten. I was half stunned but not at all surprised. I added another check mark to my own personal mental tally that she seemed to occupy in my mind.

"I think you'll do just fine today. You don't need any extra help." I reached for my notes and gave them one last glance.

"Shame." She pouted playfully.

I tossed the pages back on the desk. "You know, usually, I'm a less is more kind of girl, but never to be forgotten sounds like the start of some great story, a prophecy or something."

"The cost of the free pass was never to be forgotten," she proclaimed.

"I guess you'll never know." I stuck out my tongue and her gaze remained fixed on my mouth.

After we handed in our papers, we spent the remainder of the class scribbling out notes and making future plans.

Drew's having a party next Saturday. Can you come? Lauren passed me the sheet of paper and I looked at it strangely.

He didn't invite me.

Last time I checked it was my house as well. Come and keep me company.

She passed the note back in my direction and I pretended to hem and haw over my decision.

I'll have to think about it, I finally wrote after watching her impatiently squirm for a couple of minutes.

Pretty please? she replied.

I looked down at her last scribble and pretended to feign disinterest, but I eventually conceded and nodded in agreement.

Her arms were around my neck pulling me in for another awkward hug as the students around us huffed in irritation at the distraction.

There was no chance that I would miss out on that party.

CHAPTER NINETEEN

Patricia leaned over my desk, her arms wrapped around a stack of books, ready for her next class.

"I had fun last week."

"Yeah, me too. It was nice."

"Just nice?" She bit down on her lower lip.

I leaned a little closer. "Did you know that another word for nice is *gratifying*." I smiled. "Don't knock the word nice. I'm just being polite and proper because I'm at work." My gaze traveled around the library to emphasize my point but got stuck on a curious blonde standing only a few feet away, who appeared to be impatiently eavesdropping on our conversation.

"Would you like to grab coffee tomorrow afternoon between my classes?" she asked.

I was only half paying attention and it wasn't fair to Patricia. I turned back. "That'd be *nice*." Unfortunately, when I emphasized the last word, it wasn't for Patricia's benefit or her ears and I immediately regretted it.

"Great, I'll come and grab you when I'm done." She pulled the books away with her and had to sidestep the nosy blonde in the process.

I followed her until she approached the exit doors and passed through them. I didn't acknowledge Lauren. I purposely ignored her approach, the soft clearing of her throat, and the fingernails that drummed on the top of the woodgrain. After I released a long love-struck sigh, I turned my attention back to the front of my desk. "Next time feel free to perch right on top and then you can hear our entire conversation word for word," I said with a dashing smile.

"Things are getting serious between you two." She waited for me to fill in the blanks.

"It's nice," I said and her look turned sour. Little did she know that Patricia and I had only shared a kiss, which despite my earlier banter, wasn't anything to write home about. I shrugged. "Why waste time? Life's short and we're both single." I looked down to Lauren's outstretched hand which clutched a piece of paper. "What are you doing here?"

"It's a library, Kate."

"What are *you* doing *here*?" I asked again, in no mood to play her games.

"I can't find my book." She handed me a scrap of paper with a call number on it.

I tossed the paper back at her the second it touched my fingertips and pointed in her direction. "You knew the Dewey Decimal System fifteen years ago and you know it now. 'Oh, Kate, how will I ever find my books?'" I mocked as I batted my eyelashes.

"Worked like a charm back then, didn't it?" she said smugly. "You fell all over yourself helping me find my books when we first met." She smirked.

"There's your version of events and then there's the truth. Your memory of that time is severely distorted, and as for right now, the only thing we need to discuss is if you have any overdue fines." I took the library card from her other hand, scanned it and squinted at the screen. "*Everything After Is Us* was due back three days ago." I brought up my browser and did a quick Internet search. I shook my head as I looked up at Lauren. "You're still a sucker for lesbian romance. You owe the library seventy-five cents for your tardiness." I put her card down on the counter and held out my hand. "We take cash, credit, or your soul," I said ominously.

"I want us to be friends again."

"*Friends?*" I said slowly as I blinked in shock. "We were never friends. We were a lot of other things, some of them were *nice*… But we weren't friends."

"So, we just do this?"

"Yeah." I nodded my head. "We do this."

"I'm sorry that I hurt you."

I expelled a long unsteady breath. Propriety and politeness had left the building long ago. I pushed Patricia away but was ready to go ten rounds with Lauren, damned who bore witness. "You didn't," I said softly. I offered a sad smile as a peace treaty. "I hurt myself. It was my stupidity to get involved with someone who was married. I don't blame you for lying to me."

"Not everything is as black and white as you think it is. It's obvious you blame me. You've changed. You're very angry now."

"Don't you mean extra sarcastic? Isn't that what the kids call it these days? *Extra?*"

"It feels like anger."

I shrugged because it was true, wasn't it?

"Is this anger because of me, us?"

"*Us?*" I looked at her baffled. "There was never an *us*." I realized at that moment that I had raised my voice at work. My next words were a hushed, hurried whisper. "You don't know who I am anymore. I have no idea who you are. If our daughters weren't friends, I'd have nothing to say to you other than reminding you of your overdue fines." I held out my hand again to emphasize my point.

"Sue me." She picked up her card and walked away.

"I take library fines very seriously, Ms. Dawson," I called after her. "Don't make me revoke your library privileges."

Just like that, I fell back into an old familiar pattern with Lauren. On one hand, it made me feel warm and comfortable, and on the other hand, pure never-ending nausea, because I didn't know what was going to happen next.

I left work a few hours later, and I was halfway through the quad when I saw him coming. I looked skyward and silently cursed to the universe. "Trying for the trifecta?" I muttered to the cosmos.

"I heard you were back in town."

"Wanted to come and see if the rumors were true, did you?"

Drew sneered as he sized me up. We had all aged and developed lines and grey hair, but Drew's were especially pronounced, making him look menacing.

"Don't you just love small towns? Congratulations on the new baby by the way," I offered sincerely.

"Came back to take a run at my new wife?"

"Drew…" I wanted to make peace with him, but the longer he stood there trying to intimidate me, the less I cared about easing him or his ego. "You know I prefer blondes."

"Go fuck yourself, Kate."

"Noted."

"Don't you have something to say to me?"

"One thing about small towns, gossip sure does travel quickly. I'm not one to judge, especially about this, but from what I hear, you're throwing stones from a glass house. Do you need an apology from me? Because I'll give you one, and maybe I should have done it years ago. I'm sorry for what we did to you. It was wrong. But to act the way you're acting… You're no better than me."

"You have no idea the lives you've ruined."

"We'll now you're just being dramatic."

"And you don't even care."

"She picked you!" I yelled, because I was fed up and didn't care anymore. "She picked you, you lucky bastard, and you fucked it up."

He watched me for the longest time, waiting for me to say something else, but when I didn't he finally spoke. "She hasn't told you, has she?"

"We don't talk. Despite what you think, I didn't come back for Lauren. I came for Jack. The universe is apparently playing this sick joke on all of us because it's decided to make our daughters friends. Abbie is a lovely girl, and I guess you're fifty percent responsible for that, so kudos… I think that's all I have to say to you."

I walked away and he never said another word.

CHAPTER TWENTY

Fifteen years earlier

A couple of days before the party, Lauren traipsed up and down the basement aisles with me. It was late and thankfully almost time to close for the night. It was completely empty, just me, Lauren, and the microfiche. "You know, you don't have to stay with me," I said as I pushed the trolley.

"I don't like the thought of you walking home this late at night. Why won't you drive your car?" She picked up another book from my cart and put it in its proper place on the shelf.

"I like walking home at night. It gives me an opportunity to clear my head."

"I don't like it."

It was a battle that was already lost and I knew it. Even if she didn't join me on my evening rounds, she would always show up at the end of my shift, parked outside the library waiting for me. I often wondered what she said as she was leaving her house. Was she honest with him? Before I could stop myself. "What do you say to him?"

"Who?"

"Your husband. Doesn't he ask you where you wander off to at eleven o'clock at night?"

"Well, if he's there, I tell him that I'm driving a friend home."

"That doesn't bother him?"

"Should it?"

I shrugged. "I might have something to say about it, if I had a wife." I made sure to add the last part. "Not the first time, or the second, but definitely the third time."

"And what would you say to her?"

"It doesn't matter."

"You started the conversation. What would you say?"

"Get your ass back to bed, I'm not done with you yet."

It took a second for my words to sink in and when they did, we both laughed.

"You would never say that!"

"No, but I'd think it."

"I'd pay a small fortune to know what you're thinking sometimes."

"It's not worth anything."

"I disagree. Seriously, what would you say?"

"I don't know…" I swallowed my trepidation. I knew that I should hold my tongue, but I couldn't. "I'd ask her to think about where she really wanted to be."

She didn't say anything for the longest time, and when she did, it was a whisper. "You know, you never told me where to make out."

I knew she was deflecting and simply trying to get out of the conversation, but it didn't stop me from instinctively looking for the nearest exit because it felt like I was on the cusp of an emergency. I didn't know what to say, so I said the first thing that popped into my mind. "I really don't want to stumble across you and Drew getting hot and heavy on a night shift."

For the moment it was the reality check that we both needed, because the mere mention of his name did enough to dampen whatever mood had been created. It remained with us until I finished my shift and we were halfway through the drive back to my apartment. She parked under a street light and shut off the car. She took off her seatbelt and softly drummed her hands against the bottom of the steering wheel. I took off my seatbelt, but made no move to leave. Instead, I turned slightly toward her, waiting for her to do or say something.

"I know it's strange, but I feel like we have a connection."

I started to argue but I couldn't. She was right. We did. I was in the process of developing a strong connection with a married straight woman and I didn't know how to stop it, and I didn't know if I wanted too.

"We're good friends," I offered.

She shook her head and finally turned to me. "I don't even know how you smell, but I know that I like it."

"How is that even possible? We're around each other all the time." Despite her own proximity, I could already smell the lavender from memory.

"I've never let myself..."

And there it was. Proof of her brilliance and something else that I didn't want to acknowledge. Why didn't I think of that? How many sleepless nights could I have avoided as lavender fairies danced through my head?

Instead of doing anything to dampen this moment, I inserted my foot firmly back into my mouth. "I smell like fresh cotton."

She moved from her seat until she was inches from me.

"What are you doing?" I whispered.

A curious expression crossed her features and held me in place. She leaned forward and rested her head against my shoulder. Her nose pressed into my collarbone and she inhaled deeply. I remained absolutely still. I was terrified at what she would feel, the absence of a heartbeat, as she had silenced mine completely. Her eyes slowly blinked and she tilted her head to the side. "I like it."

I'd never had three of the simplest words knock the wind completely out of me. I instinctively licked my lips and swallowed down the lump that had lodged itself in my throat.

"Do you want to smell me?" she asked, like it wasn't the strangest thing that she had ever said, but casually like she was asking me to coffee.

I shook my head, desperate to remove myself from this strange stupor. I couldn't verbalize my words, not yet trusting my voice.

"Why not?"

I held her gaze for a beat longer than I should have, getting lost in the feel of her head on my shoulder and the fact that if I just leaned forward fractionally, I could trace the soft lines of her lips with my own. "You smell like lavender and something else…" A voice that wasn't my own spoke out.

A shy blush spread across her features and the crease in her upper lip that resembled a chaste smile would be imprinted on my memory until I had my last coherent thought and left this world. "Do you want to know what the something else is?"

"*No.*" I truly didn't. If I knew the special combination, I would have filled my apartment with the scents until they consumed me completely, and then I would have avoided them at all costs, when it went south. I could live in a world without lavender, but I couldn't live without the summer or an autumn breeze, because I was starting to come to the realization that she was all of those things and so much more. *No.* It felt like a misguided game of Russian Roulette with only me holding the gun. Just another way to slowly destroy myself. *No, thanks.*

"How come?"

I moved away, breaking the contact until I was against the car door. I sighed into the quiet confines of the space that existed between us. "Lauren… I shouldn't know that you smell like lavender to begin with."

She had never told me, not once. She just always seemed to be in my personal space or I was in hers. It was more than I wanted to say. It was an acknowledgment, an admission. It was me prying open the window just a fraction, and when I did, that damn scent of lavender drifted in.

CHAPTER TWENTY-ONE

After our last encounter, where I was a jackass incarnate, I decided to try and smooth things over with Lauren. *For the girls' sake.* I stood in front of the Steam Bean and felt more nervous than I had in years. As I pushed through the doors, the air smelled and tasted the same; it was Lauren and coffee, a perfect combination. As I forced myself further into the shop, the cosmetic changes were obvious. She had updated most of the décor and replaced the espresso machine. It was less of a college hang-out and more of a comfortable café where you could relax well into the evening hours.

I walked up to the front and looked at the menu. To my surprise, *Chocolate-vanilla Latte*, was written under specialty drinks. My mouth immediately watered. I hadn't had anything as good in fifteen years. I could see Lauren off to the side doing what looked like inventory. She looked up at me when I approached the cash register. Her gaze held mine for a second and then she became engrossed once again in her paperwork.

"You put it on the menu," I said more to myself than her.

"What?" She looked up from her clipboard.

"Chocolate-vanilla latte." I pointed to the menu.

"A long time ago."

I turned to her employee, a young woman, who was no doubt one of the students. "I'll get a large chocolate-vanilla latte." I pulled out some money and put it down on the counter.

"She can't have that," Lauren's command rang out and took me by surprise.

"Why?" Both her employee and I asked at the same time.

"I'm not the barista today."

"It's on your menu." I pointed to the chalk scrawl, which I knew without a doubt was hers.

She shrugged and turned to her employee in the most commanding voice that she possessed and said, "She can't have it." There wasn't an ounce of room for argument. The employee took a step back from the cash register, clearly wanting no part of our exchange.

But just because she was a coward, didn't mean that I was. "Are you kidding me? I'm a paying customer." I pushed my money forward on the counter.

"I'm not on today. You can't have it." We both knew that she was in the wrong, but she held firm to the pile of dirt that she had just kicked up. "You can have anything else," she said, trying to pacify me.

"That's discrimination," I shot back like a sullen child being told that they would not be getting ice cream today and instead were on their way to the dentist.

"On what ground?" She smirked.

I shot daggers at her as I recalled all of my legal training, but I still came up empty-handed. "When I figure out one, you'll hear from my lawyer."

"I can't wait to hear from you, Kate," she said in a flirtatious voice and I almost fell backward. "Can we get you anything else?"

I shook my head as I tried to find my footing and said the only thing that came to mind. "No, your coffee sucks anyway."

"Go to the chain then. Oh, wait, we both know that you won't do that."

"Don't act like you know me."

"Don't I?"

"I'll make my own coffee. Thanks for nothing."

"You don't still drink that instant crap, do you?"

She knew exactly how to get under my skin and push all of my buttons. She was a master at getting a rise out of me and I hated it. After all this time, I absolutely detested it. I did the most immature thing that I could think of: I flipped her off, turned toward the door, hesitated and turned back around. "Your coffee doesn't suck." What I meant to say was, *please stop pushing me, please let the past lie*, but for as much guts as I thought I possessed, I didn't have those particular ones.

She laughed as I left the shop.

The next morning, not to be outdone by Lauren, I knocked loudly on the window pane of the Steam Bean to get her attention. When she finally looked in my direction, because her customers had all turned around, I held up my travel mug and pointed at it with a large grin. Take that, I wanted to yell. I waited for her to acknowledge defeat but it never came, and when she winked at me, like she had done a hundred times before, it was disarming and I felt like I had made a terrible mistake. Unfortunately, I couldn't backpedal now. "Jokes on you," I mouthed and took a satisfying sip of my instant.

I crossed the street and walked into the library feeling confident and ready to start a new day. It was going to be a good one. I could feel it with my early morning victory still pumping through my veins. As I neared my desk, my stomach bottomed out because there sat a take-out cup from the Steam Bean, with my name written in a familiar cursive and an exclamation mark with the upside-down heart for a period.

When I grasped the cup, it was still hot. I brought the cup to my nose and inhaled deeply. The aroma of the drink was unmistakable. I sighed and placed it down on the desk. I sat in my chair and looked at the steam as it rose from the small hole in the lid. I pushed it away, picked up my travel mug and screwed off the lid. I brought it to my nose and inhaled the scent of instant. It smelled comfortable and familiar, but as hard as I tried to push the scent into my head and remove the aroma of

Lauren's concoction, I couldn't do it...she remained. My gaze flashed to the white and blue cup. I closed my eyes and screwed the lid back onto my travel cup.

On my very first break, I walked back into the Steam Bean. Lauren was behind the counter fixing a coffee, but she looked up at me and smiled. "Enjoy your coffee?" she asked sweetly, and the flirtatiousness that was present the day before had carried over.

There was so much I wanted to say, but only one thing came to mind. "It's different. It's better. You changed the recipe."

"Slightly. I had to step up my game."

"What does that mean?"

"I made it a little more enticing for you." She winked and I bit down on my bottom lip to suppress my smile. "Remember when you told me that I smelled like lavender and something else, but you didn't want to know what the something else was?"

"Vaguely."

"You are such a liar."

I shrugged.

"The something else is now in the coffee." She smiled smugly.

I didn't want to swallow but I did, and even though the aftertaste was still present, and delicious on a whole new level, I couldn't discern the new flavor. Blast this woman!

"You want another one, don't you?" She teased.

I walked to the cash registered and dropped a handful of coins into the tip jar. The look on Lauren's face was one of slight irritation, like always, but there was amusement there as well.

I turned and headed toward the door.

"It was my treat," she called out after me.

I shook my head and walked out. When I hit the fresh air, I took a deep breath, until I could feel it in my ribs. It was like old times again and I was stupidly repeating the mistakes of my past.

CHAPTER TWENTY-TWO

Fifteen years earlier

We didn't talk about the incident in the car for the next couple of days. We ignored it completely. When class rolled around on Monday, it was like nothing had happened and we went back to our normal routine. She even pointed out different women, who she thought would be compatible for me. I was baffled given everything that had happened, but I just accepted it as the proper order of things. She joined me for a couple of shifts at the library and I popped into the shop. When the night of the party arrived, the incident in the car was the furthest thing from my mind.

After she took my coat, I stood in the threshold and surveyed the room. There was a handful of students from my program and some that I didn't recognize. Before I could move toward the kitchen, a familiar voice held me in place.

"Kate," Drew said as he approached me, considering me carefully. No doubt he was trying to figure out what the hell I was doing in his home without an invitation.

"Lauren invited me."

"I didn't know you two were friends."

"We have Women's Lit together."

He cocked his head to the side.

"On Mondays." I offered but it made no difference as the blank look on his face remained.

"She never told me."

"Well… You'll be happy to know she's the most brilliant person in class."

He shrugged and all I wanted to say was, "wrong answer," but I held my tongue.

Just before he moved onto a more interesting conversation he called out, "drinks are in the kitchen, help yourself."

"Thanks…"

When Lauren reappeared a second later, I couldn't help myself any longer. "Your husband doesn't know you're in Women's Literature."

"There's a lot of things my husband doesn't know." There was an edge to her voice that had never been present before.

"Do you want to talk about it?" I asked after a moment.

"No."

"Okay…"

After several seconds of very awkward silence, my gaze focused like a laser on the brunette in the corner of the room. I gently elbowed Lauren in the ribs. "Who's that?" I whispered as she leaned in closer.

She scanned the room. "Who?"

"Short brown hair. She's by the bookcase, admiring your collection."

"Oh," she hesitated for half-a-second. "She's not gay," she said quickly.

My lips formed into a smile even before I turned to her. "I didn't ask if she was gay. I asked who she was. Besides, I'm pretty sure she's into girls. I'll bet you five bucks."

"How do you know?"

"It's a sixth sense." I snapped my fingers. "What's her name?"

"Why?"

"So that I can go and introduce myself."

"I really don't think she's gay."

"That's my problem, not yours. *Name*?" I waited impatiently.

After a beat, she finally said, "Morgan. She's one of Drew's friends."

"Don't you just love women with gender-neutral names?" I winked. "How do I look?"

She gave me a once over, looked away and shrugged. "You've got this serious, pouty lip thing going on and your dimple is very pronounced tonight. I don't know if that works for women."

My mischievous grin was gone and replaced with a curious one. "Well, I've never had one describe me quite like that." I laughed lightly. "But I'll take it." I undid one of the top buttons on my shirt and Lauren's gaze quickly flashed to my chest.

"Why'd you do that?" she asked, but she never looked at me directly. Instead she was still focused on the small expanse of skin.

I cleared my throat and her gaze met mine. "I'm highlighting my *assets*."

"You don't need to do that. You're going to be a lawyer for God's sake."

"I can't lead with that. I'll come across as a huge jerk. 'Hi, Morgan, I'm going to be a lawyer, would you like to sleep with me?'"

"You want to sleep with her?" she asked so quickly that it made my neck snap. She waited for my answer, her mouth slightly open.

I shrugged. "She's cute. It's not like I've got that many opportunities here. I try and capitalize when and where I can. I'm not like you." I gestured up and down with my hand. "I can't have anyone I want."

"I can't have anyone I want, trust me," she said quietly.

"I meant if you weren't married."

"I could have anyone I wanted if I wasn't married?"

"Yes, Sherlock."

"Why?"

I leaned away. "Have you seen you?" I gave her a quick once over to emphasize my point. "Look in a mirror sometime."

"Even women?"

"If that was your thing, yes. You'd have to hire me to be your bodyguard. You'd be lesbian catnip. I'd have to beat them off with a stick and redirect them my way." I winked, but she didn't seem amused. "I'm going in. Wish me luck."

"No," she said under her breath, but I caught it anyway.

"I don't need it."

I sauntered over to the bookcase, head up, back and shoulders straight until I was standing beside Morgan. I reached for a random title on the shelf and flipped it over in my hands pretending to be engrossed in the print. After a second, I turned to my left and she was watching me. "Have you ever read this one?" I flashed the front of the book in her direction.

She glanced at the title and shook her head. "I don't think so. What's it about?"

I flipped the book over, glanced at the title and then gazed at Morgan. "I don't have a clue, but I'd be more than happy to read it to you while we're lying in my bed," I said confidently. "We can start our own private book club. Clothed, semi-nude, naked, the choice is yours." I grinned.

When she smiled it was warm like she was inviting me to a naughty tea party, but instead of tea, we'd sip a fine whiskey out of Grandmother's good china. The look, the promise, was exhilarating.

"Morgan, right?" I asked shyly, already liking how it sounded leaving my lips.

"Have we met?" She looked at me carefully, no doubt trying to place me.

"No, but I've heard good things about you." I caught my ever-increasing smile and tried to temper my expression, downplaying the parade of possibilities that undoubtedly had crossed my features.

"Really?"

I put my right hand over the book and held it up in the air. "I swear on the book club. What should we call it? Easy Reads?"

"I'm not joining anything until I know your name."

"Kate." I extended my hand. "Someone once told me that when I introduce myself, I should lead with the fact that I'm going to be a lawyer, but that's lame and pretentious, so I lead with the book club. Don't forget to ask about the exclusive benefits that come with membership."

"Like what?" She bit down on her lip.

"Like—"

At that moment, Lauren walked over and took the book from my hands. "Have you guys met?" she asked dismissively. "Morgan, this is Kate. She's in the law program." She turned back to me. "Morgan's in engineering."

"I know." I nodded my head slowly, but my gaze was fixed on Morgan. "We just did that part but it was more fun." I turned and punched Lauren gently on the shoulder. "Thanks, though."

"I'll be right back." Morgan smiled and placed her hand on my forearm.

I mentally threw my hands up in the air, signaling a touchdown.

"I just want to grab a drink. Do you want anything?"

"No, thanks. I have my car here. I'm a one and done girl, but only with drinking and driving. With other things…" I wiggled my eyebrows suggestively.

She squeezed my arm. "I'll think of a name for the book club."

"Fantastic. I can't wait to hear it." When Morgan was out of earshot, I turned toward Lauren. "I got this."

"Are you sure? It didn't look like it."

"Pretty *damn* sure. This isn't straight dating. We don't really bullshit one another."

"Really? It looked like you needed a hand."

"Like the hand that was just on my arm?" I raised my eyebrows. "Because I agree. I definitely need *that* hand. She's about to come up with a name for our very naked book club. Actually, that's the perfect name! Our Very Naked Book Club. Can I borrow this?" I grabbed the book back from Lauren's hands. "I may need it as a prop." I quickly scanned the jacket. "Blah, blah, blah." I stopped reading and looked intently at the words near the bottom. "Sapphic romance…" I looked up at Lauren who was a deep shade of red. "Why is your husband reading lesbian romance?" I grinned like the devil.

She snatched the book from my hands and hid it behind her back. "She's a little messy when she gets drunk," Lauren blurted as she deflected and I attempted to reach for the book.

"I don't get girls drunk, so that's not going to be a problem. Let's forget about that for a second. What the hell have you been reading?" I lunged for the book and she quickly backed toward the wall. As I struggled to get the book, I pressed completely into her. She maneuvered so the book was just out of reach. It was the closest we had ever been up to that point in time.

I couldn't focus long on our proximity, only a second, because when Lauren spoke next, I froze. "If I let you see the book, will you tell me about the benefits of the book club?"

"Huh?" I stammered out and loosened my grip on her arm, but she was still pressed against me, her warmth seeping into me.

"I want to know about the benefits," she said again and my ears burned. Her eyes sparkled with a hint of longing that should never have been there. It both thrilled and startled me.

I immediately loosened my grip and completely backed away when I realized our position, when her words sunk in just a little bit deeper. "You're really funny, you know that?"

"I'm not –"

But she stopped when Morgan reappeared with a beer in hand. The spark in Lauren's eye was gone and she quickly moved away from us with the book cradled tightly against her chest.

As the night wore on, there were four unmistakable truths that I couldn't shake. The first was that Morgan was interested in me. The second was that Lauren knew it too, as her ears and eyes followed us around the apartment, but she wasn't the only one who had a wandering eye. As hard as I tried to be engaged with Morgan, I couldn't stop myself from looking for Lauren and becoming completely captivated in how she moved in her space, who she spoke with and how she looked when she snuck a glance in my direction. Morgan was sweet, kind, gay, and above all else—not married. But when we spoke or she touched me, it felt like something was missing. The third truth,

Lauren was right: Morgan was a messy drinker. But the most important truth of all… The married couple didn't appear all that happy together. They barely interacted, and when they did, it was usually him demanding something of her. Each time it happened it added to my growing agitation.

I went into the office and picked up our coats off the desk. Just as I turned, Lauren was in the threshold. "Are you leaving already?"

"I'm going to take her home. She's had too much to drink."

"I'll get her a cab."

"No, it's fine."

"She should take a cab home," Lauren insisted.

"I've got it. I only had one glass hours ago. I'm good."

I went to move past her but stopped when she said, "Are you going to sleep with her?" She quickly pressed her lips together tightly when I glared in her direction.

"In her state?" I waited for a response that never came. "I'm not going to dignify that with a response." I moved past her and back into the party.

The insistent knocking on my door came late, but I wasn't sleeping. After dropping off Morgan and making sure she got into her apartment, I came home and replayed the events of the evening. I should have been focused on meeting someone new, but my thoughts kept rewinding to the feeling of Lauren in my arms as I struggled to get the book from her hands and her very deliberate words, "Tell me about the book club."

When I finally opened my door because the knocking was never going to end, Lauren stood, hand half raised, looking desperate.

"What's wrong?"

It looked like she was going to tell me, but the explanation never came. "Can I come in?" she finally asked, after it looked like she was warring with herself.

"Of course, what's wrong?" A million scenarios played out in my mind.

"Is Morgan here?" she asked as she walked in, her gaze fixed on my bed.

I immediately reached for her shoulder to halt her progress and she turned toward me. "Lauren, I don't know what kind of person you think I am, but I would never take advantage of someone who's drunk."

She closed her eyes and released a deep breath. A silence settled in the room as she gently shook her head. It was so subtle that I almost missed it. "I think… Something is happening. I have these *thoughts* when I'm around you." She paused. "I'm attracted to you," she said in a slight whisper, "and I think…" The words caught in her throat as she opened her eyes to look at me, and it was nothing but vulnerability for miles. "…that you're attracted to me too."

My ears roared. How many times had I dreamt of this scenario? However, not once was I completely stunned into silence and inactivity by her admission. The longer she stood rooted, the more it appeared she was starting to shake, but it was me. I needed to say something. I swallowed the heartbeat that threatened to spill out of my chest and said the only thing that mattered at that moment. "You're married," quickly left my lips as I replayed her words over and over.

"You said I could have anyone I wanted."

"Stop." I shook my head. This wasn't happening. This couldn't be happening.

"I want you."

"You're married," I repeated, more to myself than her.

"You've never thought about me?" She looked at me intently, searching for something that she would never find since I had locked it away.

"Go home," I said forcefully and pointed to the door.

"Is this because you have hang-ups with bisexuals?"

I was immediately taken back. "I don't have hang-ups with bisexuals. Where the *hell* did that comes from?"

"Because you're a lesbian."

"What the hell does that have to do with anything?"

"I read somewhere that lesbians don't like being with bisexuals."

I placed my hands over my chest. "I've dated and slept with women who were bi. That's not a hang-up." I looked intently at Lauren and she looked lost. "I'm going to go out on a limb and feel free to cut it right off, but if you're coming to the realization that you may be bisexual… that's amazing," I said with all sincerity. "I'm so happy for you. We can plan your first gay brunch." I smiled and then it turned serious again. "Please know that I have no issues with you being bi. I'm unbelievably proud of you. My *only* issue is the fine print on your marriage certificate."

"You don't feel anything?" she asked, her doe eyes pleading. Bambi's mom had nothing on Lauren. "You look at me like… I don't know, your eyes linger. I've never had another woman, anyone, do that before; look at me like you do."

I mentally slapped myself. I closed my eyes. Despite my best intentions not to be obvious, it was not lost on the one person that it absolutely had to be lost on. "I'm sorry."

"I'm not, Kate. I just don't know what to do with it."

"There's nothing to do with it. You're married. That's the only thing either one of us needs to know. I'll be better. I'm not going to do anything, Lauren. You have nothing to worry about. I would never do anything to make you feel uncomfortable."

"You not doing anything is making me uncomfortable. I lay awake at night and think of what it would be like to kiss you."

Every fiber in my being wanted to embrace that last sentence for as long as I could, but I wasn't allowed those thoughts. "You need to leave." I pointed again to the door, but it was less forceful this time.

"Don't you think about it?" she asked, but I said nothing.

She had laid her cards out on the table and mine were still clutched tightly to my chest. As the seconds ticked by, the relief that initially crossed her features with her revelation was replaced by a wave of apprehension. As she turned for the door, I did the one thing that I would no doubt regret for the rest of my life.

"*Soft*," I said quietly, as my mind, words, and ethics betrayed me. "It would be soft." I swallowed the rest of my words. I had said enough for the night, and possibly a lifetime.

She stopped walking and faced me. "I don't want you to see her."

I inhaled deeply at the realization that I had just contributed to unlocking Pandora's box. "You have no right to ask me that. You need to leave."

"It will kill me to see you with her."

"Her or any other woman?" I asked, but I already knew the answer.

"It will kill me."

"Like me seeing you with him?" I asked with a pointed tone. I shook my head and a bitterness that I didn't realize existed in my chest made its presence known. "You never die... I'm still here."

* * *

When I walked into class on Monday, Lauren was already seated. Waiting on my desk was a large cup from the Steam Bean with my name on it in Lauren's scrawl. She gave a quick smile as I sat down, and before I could remove anything from my bag, she leaned in. "I'm sorry about the other night. I never should have told you who you could see." She lowered her voice and leaned in closer. "I have these feelings and I don't know what to do with them."

"You don't do anything with them. *We* don't do anything with them," I stressed, because that was the one, absolute, universal truth. You don't cheat. I wasn't going to put myself in that kind of situation. I wasn't going to be the *other*. There was no mathematical equation that equaled us being together as long as she was married.

"I want you in my life," she pleaded.

"And I'm here, as your *friend*," I clarified with a half-smile.

Everything was starting to feel like half when it came to Lauren, like I was only living half of my life, because I could only have half of her.

She broke me from my thoughts. "You think about me too," she urged in a hushed whisper.

I shook my head quickly and narrowed my eyes. "We need to forget it. I never should have said that. It wasn't fair to either of us. It doesn't matter because there's a fundamental detail that we can't ignore: *you're married*," I whispered harshly to make my point abundantly clear.

She turned away quickly and faced the front of the room, leaving a biting chill in her absence.

"Thank you for the coffee," I said as warmly as I could muster, hoping to thaw some of the tension.

She reached down and squeezed my free hand that was resting on top of my thigh and held it tightly.

One Mississippi…

Two Mississippi…

Three Mississippi…

I counted in my head.

I whispered in her ear. "I wish it were different." I closed my eyes and resisted the urge to inhale her scent, and focused on the task at hand. This needed to stop now. "You can't hold my hand," I stressed softly. Rejecting Lauren tasted like acid on my tongue and it burned straight to my stomach.

Four Mississippi…

Five Mississippi…

"*Lauren*," I warned as gently as I could.

She sighed and took her hand back. After a moment she reached for her pen and a piece of paper, scribbled out a note and pushed it toward me.

i know where i want to be.

i want to be with you.

I read and re-read the note. I wanted to digest the words, but there was one problem that I couldn't ignore: she was still married.

CHAPTER TWENTY-THREE

After that first cup of coffee, the peace treaty coffee, it was hard, if not altogether impossible not to find myself at her shop day after day. I was going for the latte, I convinced myself every morning on my first break, but I lingered throughout the morning because of Lauren.

"I didn't get to tell you before, but I like what you've done with the place. It's less impoverished. Less… I've only eaten ramen noodles for a week and shabbier chic."

"We make a mean ramen soup here."

"Probably the only reason they can also afford to buy the coffee." I winked.

"So," she wiped her hands on a white towel hanging off her shoulder. "What can I get you?"

I looked up at the chalk. "Depends." I leaned across the counter. "Can I get whatever I want on the menu?" I didn't mean for it to sound suggestive but it did, and Lauren being Lauren, jumped all over it.

"That was never a problem before." She wiggled her eyebrows.

"I'm not flirting with you. Can I please have a large chocolate-vanilla latte? Or are you going to make up some ridiculous excuse as to why I don't get to have one today?"

We always came back to this exchange, like that one moment a few weeks ago, had eased the tension between us and gotten us here. She could flirt if she wanted and I could engage if I wanted, but more often than not, I just rolled my eyes and ignored her.

"It's your lucky day because my barista had a presentation this morning and it's just me."

"My lucky day indeed," I teased, but I made sure that it didn't come across as suggestive this time. One suggestive comment was already enough for the day.

I pulled out my cash but she ignored me, just like she had done every other time before and just like every other time, I let the money fall into the tip jar.

"You know, with the number of tips that I've left you over the years, you could have traveled the world, twice over."

She turned as she fiddled with the knobs on the machine. She considered me for a moment, like she was debating with herself, but then the words came out. "Imagine what I could have done without a fifteen-year absence."

I swallowed down her comment and it burned as it passed my windpipe. There was no retort from me. No smartass response. There was nothing I could say. She wanted me to acknowledge that I wasn't the only one that felt pain when I left Renfrew. I didn't care about her pain, not then and not in this moment. Fifteen years without seeing her was unbearable, but if I had to watch her every day with him, it would have destroyed me. Leaving was the only way to survive.

She finished my latte and slid it across the counter.

I picked up the warm cup and brought it to my lips for a quick sip. I smiled at the familiar taste. "Thank you."

She turned back to clean off the machine.

"I'll see you tomorrow?" I asked but there was no reply when I left the shop.

CHAPTER TWENTY-FOUR

Fifteen years earlier

I circled the perimeter of the third floor until I confirmed that I was all alone. I walked back down the aisle to the second case, bottom shelf, last book and there it was. An oversize orange hardcover book on Minimalism, stuck between books on the Spanish Inquisition. Just as I went to pull it from the stacks Lauren called out, "There you are."

"You're just in time." I held up the orange hardcover.

"For what?" she asked and eyed the book in my hand.

"The book bandit strikes again."

"That's where they leave it?"

"Every time." I turned back to the book. "You don't belong in the Spanish Inquisition." I sat down on a nearby stool and looked up at Lauren with the book on my thighs. "Now for the exciting part." I slowly flipped open the cover, revealing my note from the last exchange, but nothing else was written, just my poem:

Roses are red
Violets are blue

This book is out of order
And so are you.

"No response." I quickly flipped through all of the pages and sighed.

"Maybe they don't even open it. Maybe it's an OCD thing for them."

I brought my hand under my chin as I gazed up at her. "Interesting theory." I peeled off my note and took out a new one.

"What are you doing now?"

"I always leave a new note and then take this baby back up to the fourth floor where it belongs." I scribbled out a quick note and stuck it back inside the front cover.

"What did you write?"

"Is this an OCD thing? You can tell me." I stood up and dropped the book on my trolley for later.

"Are you avoiding me?"

"No, I've just been busy," I said, trying to sound as convincing as possible. It was the truth, but it was a convenient break all the same. A tension had settled in the cracks between us after the party and the note. It felt heavy at times and prickly at others, like a bowling ball wrapped in porcupine quills. A timeout of quiet reflection while I tried to concentrate on other things seemed in order as this quagmire was starting to distract me from the rest of my life.

"Good, then you can come out for drinks on Friday. A few of us are going to the bar."

"I don't know."

"Please?" she asked, hands folded.

"Maybe, I have to see where I am with a factum that's due next week."

"Okay…but just come anyway. You have the whole weekend to work on it. I'll even help you with it on Sunday."

"Thanks, but it's not really something you can help me with. Some of us actually have to put in the effort."

"What does that mean?"

"You're brilliant. I am in awe of your ability to ace everything without lifting a finger."

"I do the work just like you."

My mouth hung open because we both knew it wasn't true.

"I'm going to send you an email with the details. We've hardly spent any time together in the last couple of weeks. I better see you on Friday."

* * *

I didn't want to go out for drinks on Friday, but Lauren's insistence got the better of me and I agreed to go out for one drink. I was foolish, lovesick, and all of the ills that come with it, because one drink turned into one dance, which turned into a second drink and a whole lot of dancing.

The deep bass of the music pulsed up from the soles of my feet into every nerve ending of my body, and at every ending, Lauren was there. Each beat felt like a different letter of Morse code trying desperately to signal a message to me as Lauren wrapped her arms around my neck. -.. .—. —. . .-. *Danger.* I ignored the warnings. I found myself in the middle of a suffocating dance floor surrounded by bodies that moved and swayed. It was the last place that I wanted to be, but as the music blared and the strobe light flickered, each flash illuminated a different part of Lauren's body, and it was the only place that I needed to be.

I tried to keep a rhythm, but my mind was a thousand tiny flashes of light as Lauren moved around me. I tried to gather my crumbling resolve as Lauren gracefully moved behind me, but my breath caught in my throat when her arms circled my waist and her body pressed against me. I shivered at the contact.

"You drive me *crazy* when you look at me like that," she whispered.

I closed my eyes and shook my head, but no words left my lips. I didn't pull away from the contact. My mind kept flashing back to her note, *i know where i want to be*, and it was enough, even though I knew it was wrong. I sank deeper into the touch and leaned my head back into her neck and finally breathed.

When the music changed, it was a slower pace. We moved for a second, but her lips found my ear again. "I'm going to get us a drink." Her breath nuzzled close. "Don't go anywhere."

I stayed because she asked; I felt helpless to do anything else. She moved through the sea of people and made her way up to the bar, but as soon as she did, a hand reached for her and she was pulled into a hug by a strong pair of arms. My instincts took over immediately. I was halfway toward her when I realized it was Drew. When he kissed her, I immediately turned back to the dance floor. The lights, sounds, and the proximity of every other person made me feel violently ill. I tried desperately to get air into my lungs, but they felt like they had just collapsed. As I stood in the middle of the dance floor I gasped, desperate for a breath that was back at the bar with her husband. As the room spun, I muttered over and over, "So stupid...so fucking stupid." I dashed for the nearest exit and I didn't care whose drink I spilled along the way. I needed to get out of there. As soon as I hit the fresh air, the tears stung painfully against my eyes.

When the knock came on my door an hour later, I sat on the sofa with the lights off and a 1940s jazz record spinning. I nursed a glass of my very best, only-in-case-of-emergency whiskey. I ignored the persistent knocking. I had endured all that I could for one evening. The world and the mess that had become my life could keep whirling on without me for a little while longer.

"*Kate?*" Lauren called, her voice almost frantic. She had finally opted for a different tactic. "I can hear the music. I know you're awake." She twisted the knob of the locked door. "Please let me in... *Please.*"

I said nothing as I continued to listen to the unrestricted sounds of the music coming from my record player. The notes travelled in a number of different directions. It was a perfect match to the medley of my emotions for the last few months— the highs, the lows and the dizzying undercurrent, which would surely drag me down.

"*Kate...*" In one second it was a whimper and in the next a command. "Don't shut me out."

I put down my glass reluctantly and opened the door. Lauren's arms were outstretched on either side of the wooden frame like she had taken up a post, which she wouldn't abandon anytime soon. Her head was downcast and she didn't look at me as I stood there, waiting.

"I'm sorry," she said after a few silent moments. When she looked up at me, a mixture of pain and guilt were etched on her features.

I was confused for a split second, but the emergency whiskey quickly helped with that. "For what? Leading me on?" I laughed bitterly and the words rushed out. "For kissing *your husband*? For embracing *your husband*? Insert any word and *your husband*." I practically yelled but quickly clamped my mouth shut when I came to the realization that I was just as much to blame. My shoulders sagged. "You have absolutely nothing to be sorry about." I shook my head and every ounce of bitterness was gone. "I have no right to be upset." I wanted to say something else, something that would justify the hurt and the jealousy that coursed within me up until that moment, but I was empty-handed. I wasn't allowed to feel those things, and even if I did, the responsibility rested with me. There was one universal truth that I had ignored because she made me feel everything; you don't get involved with a married woman.

"Can I come in?"

I hesitated, because after all of the events that had transpired, it made the least amount of sense. Sending her on her way, back to her husband, was the only option.

"Kate... *please*. I don't want to do this in your hallway."

The longer I thought about it, doing this in the hallway for all of my neighbors to hear was absolutely out of the question. I moved from the threshold and she walked inside.

"I'm sorry," she said again and reached to cup my face.

I backed away quickly, like her touch would burn me, and after what has happened earlier in the evening, I knew it to be true. "That's a terrible idea."

"Says who?" she asked and took a step towards me.

"*Your husband*," I practically spit out. I held up my arms and she stopped in front of me. "We have to stop seeing each other. We were stupid to think that we could continue to go along the way we were. I blame myself," I said calmly, but I felt anything but.

"I meant what I wrote. I want to be with you. I'm not happy with him. I haven't been for a long time."

"What are you saying?"

"Be patient with me, please. I'm trying to figure this out."

"Then figure it out, but whatever is happening between us needs to stop until you do."

"No," she said firmly, without any room for misinterpretation. "Nothing has happened."

"Lots has happened." I pointed down at the hand that had almost touched me.

"I'm not going to stop seeing you. I feel too good when I'm around you. I'm not giving that up."

"This is headed in one direction—"

"Where's that?"

I shook my head, trying to clear the cobwebs that almost felt like a permanent fixture in my mind these days. "This doesn't end well for me."

"I don't agree. I want to be with you. Tell me that you don't want me and I'll go."

She waited and I said nothing.

She took another step toward me, and I was just barely able to put my hands up, but the gesture halted her progress.

"Dance with me. We never finished that last dance. Dance with me and I'll go."

I swallowed down the litany of objections that were on the tip of my tongue. A thousand different iterations of the word *no* appeared, but quickly vanished into nothingness. I was so incredibly weak-willed when it came to this woman. She walked past me, her arm just slightly brushing mine, and made her way to the record player. A trumpet slowly cried out and I ached as she came within a foot of me and held out her hand. "I'm not leaving until we finish that dance."

I'd liked to say that I threw her out of my apartment. I'd liked to say that my spine reinserted itself into my body. *I'd like to say* is a fantasy land where my better intentions resided, but were never found.

"This is the worst idea you've ever had," I said quietly, as I studied her outstretched hand. I finally took it in mine and wrapped my free arm around her body, bringing her within a breath of me.

It wasn't like the first time that we danced in my apartment or earlier in the evening when she danced in front of me, around me, for me. This was different. This was something completely different and I knew that I wasn't the only one who could feel it. At that moment, it felt like we were both connected, and I started to get lost in her.

"I didn't think anything would feel better than before when we were dancing, but... *This is better*," she whispered. She molded her body closer still. It was impossible to tell where she began and I ended, and no part of me wanted to figure it out anytime soon.

I let the sounds of the music and the moment wash over me completely for the briefest of seconds. My hands left the perch of her hips and slowly moved up her back in a gentle caress. When I realized what I was doing, my hands froze and I was just about to apologize.

"Don't stop," she said, breathless.

My hands moved up and down her spine as her arms looped around my neck.

"I think about you all the time." She nuzzled my ear. "I know that I shouldn't...but I can't stop. It's never going to stop," she said nonsensically as we moved. "Do you ever think about me?"

I shook my head gently in the small confines of space that she allowed me, but a traitorous, "*yes*," left my lips and a soft moan escaped hers.

"When?"

"Every other breath," I answered truthfully and mentally switched off, surrendering myself to a situation that I didn't want to be part of, but I couldn't imagine my life without.

"You know how people talk about looking at someone and just knowing? I felt that with you the first time we met." She placed a kiss on the underside of my ear and I couldn't stop the groan.

My hands left her back and trailed up her sides, so close but so far from where I wanted to be. I brushed my lips against her pulse point which pounded. When I pulled back fractionally, her eyes were closed. We stood there, the pretense of dancing long forgotten and she finally opened her eyes. "Please, kiss me."

"Where?" I whispered as I held her face in my hands.

"Everywhere. If you miss a spot, I'll know."

I leaned in and brushed my lips against hers, in a rumor of a kiss and pulled back. "Tell me to stop," I said through a shaky breath, the last threads of my restraint and sanity unraveling.

"I'm never going to tell you to stop, but…" She hesitated for a second. "I don't know how to make it feel good for you. I don't know what I'm doing."

I pulled back, expecting a punchline in her eyes, but vulnerability mixed with desire was the only thing I found.

"You know exactly what you're doing." My lips crashed into hers, over and over, unrelenting, even when we needed air, it was only for the briefest of moments. But it was too much. I was becoming light-headed and had to pull away. I rested my forehead against hers, steadying myself with my hands on her shoulders.

I searched her face to confirm that I hadn't made a huge mistake, but her eyes were closed and her lips were parted and other than the sound of her labored breathing, I couldn't discern what she was thinking, or what would happen next. The only thing I knew was that her lips were swollen from kissing me and I couldn't look anywhere else. "Lauren?"

She opened her eyes and her expression was completely unreadable. My grip on her shoulders tightened and it became a lifeline, until she spoke again. "Why did you stop kissing me?"

"Lauren–"

Two fingers rested over my lips. She shook her head. "Never stop kissing me."

My lips moved under her fingertips, but she pressed lightly against them, keeping them closed.

"Never." She removed her fingers, leaned forward and her lips brushed mine softly and slowly as she explored my mouth. I moaned from the contact and pulled her closer. The feeling of her finally being in my arms after all this time was unlike anything I had ever felt before. Her fingertips found my lips again and she traced the lines delicately, like she was worried if she moved too quickly, I would disappear. Her fingers moved down to my chin, her palm cupped my cheek briefly and then the back of her hand ran down my jaw. "You're so soft."

I reached for her hand and brought her fingers to my mouth, kissing the pads of each one. When I placed a kiss upon her pulse point, I could feel her heart racing.

"Are you sure?" I murmured into her skin and looked up.

"I wouldn't be here if I wasn't sure about this," she said but the confident words didn't match the unsteady voice that carried them.

We kissed again and when we parted, her hands twisted and turned in the fabric of my shirt. Her grip was tight and she refused to let go. Part of me wished that this desperation would never ease, and the other part just wanted the last barriers between us to vanish completely.

"I don't want to stop, but I don't know what to do. What do you want me to do?"

She was nervous and it was obvious. I took a step back and when she reached for me, I smiled, kissed her hands in a reassuring gesture and released them. I reached for the hem of my shirt as I held her gaze and pulled it over my head in one swift motion. I tossed it to the floor and stood in front of her in my bra and jeans.

"What are you doing?"

"Making sure you're not the only one who feels vulnerable." I reached for the button at the top of my jeans, unbuttoned and stepped out of them.

"Turn around."

"I'd rather not miss the rest of this…"

I quietly chuckled. "I'm not taking anything else off. You will, but not right now. Turn around. Trust me."

As soon as she did, I wrapped my arms around her. I pulled her into me, until she was flush. I rocked back and forth ever so slightly, feeling her sink into me and the longer I did it, the more I could feel her apprehension give way.

"We're in the same boat." I pushed a kiss into the nape of her neck. "You've never been with a woman before…" I released my arms fractionally and brought my hands to the top button of her shirt. I undid the first four buttons, but left the fifth one at the bottom. I brought my lips to her ear and whispered, "but I've never been with you." She squirmed. "That last button is up to you."

There was no hesitation when her fingers pushed the button through the material and her shirt parted. I eased the material from her shoulders, down her arms, and let it fall to the floor. I brought my hands to the top of her jeans but did nothing. "Help me." We undid the button together but nothing else.

I brought her flush back against me, as my hands trailed slowly up and down her arms. The feeling of her skin against mine momentarily made me dizzy. I closed my eyes savoring the feeling. On the third pass, I eased the straps of her bra off her shoulders. I wrapped one arm around her stomach and with my free hand I moved across her chest, until my hand had pushed the material from her breasts and I caressed her. I brought my lips back to her ear. "We've both got a little bit of a learning curve…"

She pushed back against me and a moan escaped. "I don't think we're in the same boat…" she said breathlessly. "I want to touch you."

"You will. Reach behind and undo your bra if you want. I don't want to let you go."

A second later, it slipped between us and I continued to caress her.

"Communication is so important, but I don't want to ask you what you want because I'd be missing out on so much. Discovering how you move, listening to you, feeling how you react." I gently rolled her nipple between my fingers and she pushed herself further into the contact. "Tell you what I want? I *need* every shudder and every breath that falls from your lips."

The groan in her chest reverberated deep inside me. "Now you decide to talk. I should have known."

I shook my head, smiled, and placed a kiss behind her ear.

"Tell you what I want? I only have needs."

"Tell me what you need."

"You. I need you."

I brought my hands to her hips and pushed her jeans down, past her thighs, until she stepped out of them and kicked them to the side.

My hand caressed gently over the thin cotton and she squirmed. "I need your help again."

She shook her head back and forth as it rested back against my shoulder. She threaded her fingers through the back of my hair. "You're doing just fine…."

"I'm not doing this without you."

With her hand on top of mine we slipped inside the cotton. The sound that pushed past her tongue and fell upon my ears made my nerve endings twist. When her hand fell away, I didn't rush. I took my time exploring every inch of her. I committed every shudder and breath to memory. When her hand came back a few moments later trying to guide me, I bit down on her ear softly. "I thought you didn't want to help."

"Please touch me."

"I am…"

She pushed against my hand. "Kate, I need you to touch me."

I let her guide us again, and when I finally touched her, a desperation that we had both been holding onto for months escaped in a mingled moan. The sound was intoxicating, and I momentarily froze.

The stoic mask, the one that I always held in place, vanished completely, and it was no longer just the scent of lavender that had gotten past the guards. *I could fall in love with this woman.* And at that moment I realized that I already had.

CHAPTER TWENTY-FIVE

"You signed up for what?" I asked Jack completely dumbfounded.

"The school play."

"Why on earth would you do that?" Never in her previous ten years had she shown any interest in extracurricular activities, no matter how hard I tried to push sports, the arts, or even ballet.

"Because Abbie wanted too."

I internally shook my head but didn't let it show.

"And what exactly are you going to be?"

"The second goat."

"Is Abbie the first goat?"

"No, she's the donkey." Jack huffed like she had already told me.

"Isn't your class a little young for *Animal Farm*?"

"*Huh*?"

"Never mind."

* * *

Lauren approached my desk with a pile of something clutched tightly in her hands.

"What's that?" I asked.

"I'm selling tickets for the play." She passed me the booklet and I took a quick glance. "Are you going to bring Patricia?"

"Not that it's any of your business, but it's not really official or anything. It's more…casual?"

"Shouldn't you know that?"

"It's casual," I deadpanned.

"So, one ticket then?"

I reached into my pocket for some cash. "All right, how much are they?"

"Twenty dollars."

My eyes bugged out and I moved back from her outstretched hand. "For one ticket? To a third-grade play? Patricia's definitely not coming now."

"We're trying to raise money for the field trip."

"Doesn't that seem excessive? They don't even have lighting." I picked up the stack of tickets. "Just look at these. They misspelled production. I'd rather just pay her way for the trip. I mean my daughter is a goat and yours is a donkey. They aren't even speaking roles."

"Do I need to reach into your pocket and get the money myself?"

"And have you get all hot and bothered for nothing? I'll spare you." I pulled out a couple of twenties and handed one to her. "Have you bought your ticket yet?"

"Not yet."

I handed her the other twenty without thinking. "There we go. I just bought two tickets." I beamed proudly.

"Are you asking me out on a date?"

"You wish."

"We could sit together."

"We could…" I tried to think of a good excuse to suggest otherwise but came up empty.

"We should then."

"It's not a date, Lauren."

* * *

"If everyone could take their seats we're going to raise the curtain in two minutes," Jack and Abbie's teacher announced.

"What's in the bag?" Lauren asked.

"Flowers. For the girls, after the performance," I clarified.

"You're too cute."

"Shhh...don't tell anyone."

"I'm telling everyone."

"Then they'll all want me." I winked. "My daughter in a play. I never thought I'd see the day."

"Why?"

"She's just this strong, silent loner type."

"Wonder where she got that from?" She grinned.

"She would have never done this at her old school. I've encouraged this stuff, believe me, even ballet." I made a face. "She was just never interested. So, thank you."

"Why are you thanking me?"

"Because you raised a remarkable child and she's rubbing off in the best possible way on mine."

"Jack's pretty remarkable herself."

I nodded in agreement. "I don't even care that she's doing this just for a girl. The stupid things we do for women." I sighed. "There must be an anthology that I can add too."

"What's the stupidest thing you've ever done for a woman?"

I gave her a look. "You mean besides betraying all of my ethics?"

"Is it a betrayal of ethics if it's destined to happen?"

"I can see the T-shirts now. *I cheated but it was written in the stars.*" I shook my head. "I should have brought Patricia. She's not as chatty as you. She and I never get into these kinds of conversations."

"Isn't that a problem?" she asked but didn't give me time to answer. "She doesn't know how to get you to talk." She stuck out her tongue.

"I talk."

She raised her eyebrows dramatically.

The curtain made out of sheets was pulled back and the cafeteria lights were switched off. I quickly took out my phone and started recording. When Abbie came out on stage, I turned to Lauren with an excited look. When it was Jack's turn, I beamed.

"What about the nonexistent production values?" she whispered.

"Shhh…" I swatted her away.

CHAPTER TWENTY-SIX

Fifteen years earlier

The first night we were together, I truly thought it was going to be our one and only night. How foolish of me. Any reason that she could come to my place, she did. Any moment that she could sneak away, she did. I couldn't get enough. I didn't think long or hard as to what we were doing because if I did, I would have tried to convince myself to stop it. When it popped up in the back of my mind, I pushed it away. When it lingered and the uncertainty crept inside causing me to face what I was doing, her smile, her laugh, her very existence turned my head the other way.

She was splayed out beneath me, lying face down on the mattress as I moved my lips down every vertebra in her spine. It was one of my favorite things to do, mapping out Lauren's body with all of my senses. Today was touch.

"I love that *thing* you do with your mouth," she murmured into the sheets.

"What thing?"

"*Everything.*"

I smiled and leaned back on my knees. I ran my hands over the expanse of her back. It was a never-ending canvass. I traced sonnets into her lower back with my fingertips, my second favorite thing to do. It was everything that I wanted to tell her but couldn't because of our predicament.

"You're going too quickly. I can't understand when you trace the words out that fast."

"You're not supposed to understand them. They're for me, not you." I drew my tongue across the bottom of her tailbone, causing her to squirm beneath me.

"I want to have a sleepover next weekend," she said softly.

I immediately ceased my actions and my heart pounded furiously. "How are you going to manage that?" I asked as I was already busy planning out our night. "It's not snowing out."

"I'll figure it out," she said simply.

"Why do you want to have a sleepover?"

"I need to know what it's like to wake up in your arms."

I wanted to sigh but held it in. These were the comments that absolutely killed me. Half of me was ready to soar, but the other half was ready to plunge into the darkness and pray that it would be over quickly. It was always like that with her, extreme joy and pain all rolled into one; it was numbness. It was just enough to continue and just enough to cause me to look over my shoulder every other second. I closed my eyes tightly and my heart ached. I traced out *I'm never going to love anyone as I love you*, quickly and messily on her back.

"Too fast."

"It's not for you," I whispered and placed a kiss behind her ear.

* * *

She threw her arms around my neck before she sat down and her mouth lingered by my ear. "I missed you so much this weekend. I wish we had this class every day."

As the professor started to discuss the merits of chapter seven, Lauren was busy scribbling in the margins of my notebook with one hand planted firmly on my thigh.

Your body has left a permanent imprint on me. if i close my eyes, i can feel the weight and pressure of you against me. i can feel you shudder and catch your breath. i am so hungry for your thoughts and words. i want to give you everything that you want from me.

I burned the words into my memory and then studied her profile. She looked straight ahead, trying to digest what the professor was saying. I tuned out the professor's words completely, my mind and gaze focused squarely on Lauren and the small smile that played at the corner of her lips. My fingertips itched to reach out and touch her, tilt her head toward me and capture her mouth, but it was so far outside the realm of appropriateness. Instead I decided to get lost in the daydream.

She squeezed my thigh and leaned close. "You're not paying attention."

I put my hand on top of hers. "Yes, I am."

My focus remained fixed on her for the rest of class.

* * *

She kissed me deeply and then reached over to the bedside table and picked up her watch.

"*No*," I immediately reached for her, flipping her on her back, straddling her hips. "No," I said again as I pushed the watch away. "Five more minutes."

"You said that thirty minutes ago."

"And, I'll keep saying it as long as you indulge me." I leaned down and placed a kiss on the underside of her ear. "I won't see you until Monday. Do you know how long it is until Monday?" I pressed against her. "Do you know how much I'll miss you?"

"Why do you think I've indulged you? This is the worst part. I hate leaving, you know that." She turned until her lips found mine. "But I have to go."

I whimpered and rolled off until I was laying on my back beside her, my arm flung over my eyes.

"This isn't easy for me either. Leaving you is never easy."

But you leave me anyway. I ignored the sharp pain in my side. "What happened to figuring things out?" I asked because it had been on my mind constantly.

She moved until she straddled my hips. She tried to capture my gaze but I wouldn't hold her eyes. "Kate look at me... I'm not staying with him. I promise you. I just need a little more time, okay?"

She put the watch back on her wrist, strapping the thick oxblood leather across her skin. I hated it, the gatekeeper of our time together. It was the very first thing I removed when she walked into my apartment. If I didn't, she was always looking down. I was stolen moments and borrowed time, and there was never enough, even with her promises.

CHAPTER TWENTY-SEVEN

Very early that morning, the skies opened and I knew that it was only a matter of time before the schools would be closing and it was officially a snow day. Thankfully, the phone call confirming the closures made the rounds before Jack and I left for the morning. Naturally, she was excited, just as I was when I was her age, but instead of parking herself in front of the television or making the decision to go back to bed, she started to get dressed.

"Where are you going?" I asked as she layered herself in a mixture of winter clothing.

"To shovel Mr. Murphy's driveway. He said when it snowed next that I could shovel it and he would pay me."

"Why?"

"I need the money," she replied, as she tied a scarf around her neck and searched in her designated bucket of outdoor clothing for presumably a knit hat, as it was the only item she was currently missing.

"Jack, I give you an allowance. Even when you don't always do all of your chores, there it is week after week—"

"I need more money." She pulled out a green hat and pushed it down over her head, tucking her hair behind her ears.

"Why?" This was not my daughter. *Top of the morning! How do you do? Let's see how I can make some quick cash!*

"Christmas is coming."

I smiled and it touched my heart. "You always make me the best gifts."

"I want to buy something for Abbie."

My smile fell. "What am I? Chopped liver?" I called out as she made her way toward the front door. "You know, our driveway could use a shovel as well," I said, but she was already out of earshot.

I spent the next twenty minutes watching the snow swirl with a hot cup of coffee resting comfortably between my palms. I was so tickled by the events of this morning. I didn't realize what I was doing when I picked up the phone and dialed Lauren's number. "Happy Snow Day," I announced cheerfully when she picked up the phone.

"You never call me."

"I know, but I'm in a good mood today, and I didn't have anyone else to call."

"Patricia?"

"Do you want to know what my daughter is doing right this very moment?" I asked, ignoring her comment.

"What?"

"She's next door shoveling Mr. Murphy's driveway to make extra money."

"For what?"

"Because she *needs* to buy Abbie a Christmas present."

"Oh, God," the exasperated chuckle on the end of the line warmed my heart and I knew instantly why I called her; she understood. "I've already dealt with that. I told Abbie that there was a spending limit of ten dollars. She's already been saving a little extra each week from her allowance. I like Jack's ingenuity, though."

"The limit is a good idea. I'll let Jack know. Are you going into work today?"

"No. It's pretty bad out there, so I decided not to open."

"Probably a safe bet." I took a sip of my coffee and sighed comfortably.

"Instant?"

"I can feel your judgment through the phone."

"I never said a word."

"What are you drinking?"

"I've blended some beans from Brazil and Costa Rica and put them through the French press."

"Lauren Dawson, the United Nations of coffee. How does it hold up to my chocolate-vanilla latte?"

"It still needs some work."

I couldn't remember a moment over the past few months when it had been this easy between us. I didn't want it to end.

"Would I like it?"

"It's too bold for you," she teased.

"Lady, I like whiskey."

"I know you do, but you like sugary coffee drinks too."

"Whose fault is that?"

The more she laughed, the longer I stayed on the phone, chatting mindlessly with her. If we added unicorn movies and pizza to the conversation, we would have been on the verge of planning our own sleepover. But for the first time in a long time, it didn't faze me. I just enjoyed it all as the snow continued to swirl.

An hour later, my little entrepreneur trudged back inside with rosy cheeks and a twenty gripped tightly between her mitten-covered fingers. "Mom, I made twenty bucks."

"That's great." I beamed. "A good day's work, baby." I brushed some of the snow off her shoulders. "I spoke with Ms. Dawson and there's going to be a limit on the gift exchange. You can only spend ten dollars."

Jack threw her mittens in disgust. "You can't buy anything for ten dollars."

"Jack don't throw your mittens in the house." I scooped them off the floor and tossed them onto the table. "You can buy a lot of things for ten dollars. If I was in your situation, I would be able to think of a bunch of different things."

"Like what?"

But I struggled to come up with an answer. "It's not my gift. You're going to have to get creative."

"How?" she huffed.

"You could bake her some cookies. That would be well within the limit. Or cupcakes."

"That's not special." She pouted.

"Not special? I would be over the moon to get cupcakes as a present."

"Okay cupcakes, but something else, something special..." As she started to unbundle, I could tell that her mind was working on overdrive and then all of a sudden, a light bulb went off. "Can we go to the city before Christmas?"

"Why do you want to go to the city?"

"I can make her a bracelet at the bead store." She smiled proudly at her idea, and I had to admit, it was a good one.

* * *

I was as encouraging as I could be with the Christmas crowds as Jack carefully inspected every bead in the store. When she found one she liked, she would pick up an identical one and study it in relation to its counterpart to ensure she had the perfect bead. Two hours of searching and I was practically at my wit's end.

"Mom, it's nine dollars and seventy-five cents," she whined at the cash register.

"So? You're still under the ten-dollar limit."

"But I won't have enough money for cupcakes."

In order to end the madness and get the hell out of the city, I said the only thing that I could think of. "I'll spring for the cupcakes."

"Isn't that breaking the rules?"

"I guess on a technicality..." Damn my ethical parenting. "Look, I've known Ms. Dawson for a really long time. I'll make the cupcakes for her and you can give one to Abbie. That should put you squarely in the ten-dollar limit."

As we drove further away from the city, and the insanity of the Christmas season was behind us, Jack finally piped up from the passenger seat.

"How long have you known Ms. Dawson?"

"We went to school together."

"Law school?"

"No, it was college."

"Did you know Abbie's dad?"

"Only a little bit."

She was quiet for a moment and then said, "She was supposed to go to his house last weekend, but he canceled."

I sighed internally. He wasn't a bad guy. That much I knew, but the fact that he canceled on Abbie made me want to punch him in the face. I hid my dissatisfaction for Jack's sake. "Sometimes things come up and unfortunately plans need to be rescheduled. I know that he loves Abbie very much. Why all the questions?"

She yawned and I could tell that in a matter of minutes, I would be doing the rest of the drive solo as my copilot was going to be passed out.

"I like Ms. Dawson. She's the best."

"She is," I said quietly to myself.

* * *

We arrived at Lauren's and Abbie's the Friday before Christmas. Jack insisted on dressing up, which consisted of an ugly Christmas sweater with cats shooting lasers at Santa's reindeer. Every time I looked in her direction, I giggled. No matter how hard she tried to get me to join her in the ugly sweater wearing, I wasn't having any of it. But before we left the house, I grabbed a Santa hat and plopped it on my head. As we stood waiting on the porch, I instantly felt sillier in my choice of wardrobe than Jack. When Lauren answered the door, she too was dressed up for the occasion, but she was wearing anything but an ugly sweater. I was momentarily rendered speechless by the cream-colored plunging neckline and took a step back.

"Are you going out? Do we have the right night?"

"Yes, you have the right night." She smoothed her hands over her outfit.

"You dressed up…"

"Apparently, so did you," she said with a warm smile as she bit down on her lower lip.

Before she could usher us into the house, I thrust the tray of chocolate cupcakes with vanilla frosting and candy canes in her direction to try and distract myself from her smile and her infernal sweater. "Merry Christmas from your secret Santa." I winked.

Jack had already run ahead of me into the house, breaking all of my rules when it came to visiting the neighbors.

"You didn't have to get me anything," Lauren said and looked away.

Was she blushing?

"I actually did." I took a quick peek over her shoulder, to make sure that Jack was out of earshot. "Jack's gift was just under ten dollars and we figured out that one cupcake was less than twenty-five cents. So, technically Abbie can only have one and the rest are for you." If she was blushing, it disappeared with my convoluted explanation.

"You were always trying to find loopholes."

I looked over her shoulder again as I shrugged out of my winter coat. "What did Abbie get Jack?"

"Are you going to tell me what Jack got Abbie?"

"You can wait."

"Then so can you."

"Are you two ready for presents?" Lauren called to the girls. Jack ran back to the front door and got her gift from her coat pocket. I sat down on the sofa next to Lauren as the girls sat across from one another next to the Christmas tree.

"Abbie, open mine first."

When Abbie unwrapped the gift and pulled out the little bracelet with twenty different beads, she clutched it tightly to her chest and beamed at Jack. "It's so pretty."

"I picked out all the beads myself." Jack nodded excitedly as she examined it closely alongside Abbie, like she had never seen it until that moment.

"Two hours finding all those beads." I shook my head as I turned toward Lauren. "Two hours…in the city, during the holiday season, in less than ideal weather—"

She cut me off with a soft elbow to my ribs, and I couldn't help my own smile.

A moment later, Abbie placed a beautifully wrapped gift in front of Jack and looked like the most anxious person in the room. I wanted to say, "It could be socks and she's going to love it," to try and ease some of the tension from her little features, but I didn't need to worry as Jack ripped into the paper quickly and pulled out a picture frame. On the frame were the words *Best Friends Forever* with different decorations that Abbie had clearly added. In the middle of the frame was a picture of Jack and Abbie from the school play still dressed in their costumes.

Jack looked down in her lap and I knew from her smile that it was one of the best gifts she had ever received. "I love it," she cried out. "Mom, look! It's us." She held up the frame in pure bliss and my heart grew just a little. Jack pulled Abbie into a hug. "Thank you, I'm going to put it right beside my bed."

Again, I turned to Lauren. "I still can't get over how much the tickets for that play cost. Jack didn't even have a speaking role and with all the makeup they put on Abbie, you couldn't even tell it was her."

This time the elbow to my ribs wasn't so gentle.

"Mom, can we go and have cupcakes?"

"Yes." As soon as the word left my lips, they were up and out of the living room. "Please remember that almost all of those are for Ms. Dawson," I called out, but I knew it was useless.

"That was adorable." She smiled and leaned back into the couch.

Since I was trying desperately not to make Santa's naughty list, I focused on the Christmas tree and not the gorgeous woman sitting beside me. I nodded in agreement as I studied the decorations on the tree.

"Did you have that much game at her age?"

"Please… Where do you think she got it from?" I finally turned to her with a mischievous grin. It took everything not to swallow my tongue when my gaze slipped for the briefest of seconds down to her sweater. I knew I was caught and I quickly shook my head and looked away like nothing had happened.

Thankfully, she dropped it. "Think they'll save us any cupcakes?"

"Not a chance."

After a moment, Lauren got up from the couch, walked toward the tree and pulled out a gift that was sitting on top and turned back to me. It was wrapped identically to the gift that Jack had received. "Merry Christmas, Kate."

When I didn't immediately take the gift because I was shocked, she placed it in my lap.

"*What?* We aren't exchanging gifts."

"You made me cupcakes."

"That was a technicality present to get Jack out of a jam. It wasn't a real present," I whined. "You didn't even know I was going to do that. You got me a gift… I didn't get you anything."

She sat back down beside me and moved the pompom at the end of my hat from one side of my head to the other. "This was gift enough."

I looked back down at the present in my lap, desperate to hide the blush that had crept up my neck. I slowly peeled the paper back to reveal a record.

"I noticed it wasn't in your collection anymore."

"Wear and tear," I said simply, momentarily stunned.

It was the record that we had danced to on the night of the snowstorm. I knew it and so did she. What she didn't know was that after I left town, I played that record every night until it wore out, and the only reason that I couldn't bring myself to justify getting a new one was because I knew that I would do the same thing all over again, listen to it endlessly so that I could be transported back to our moment together before everything fell apart. My hand slid across the cover. "Thank you."

Later that night, when I knew Jack was asleep, I wandered downstairs, because despite my better judgment, I had to hear it. I set the needle to the third song on the album and closed my eyes. When the first notes of "I'll Be Seeing You" played, it was too much, and I immediately reached for the needle and held it suspended in the air as the disk spun. I sighed deeply and reset the needle. This time the notes didn't overwhelm me immediately. When the song ended, I reset the needle and recounted every single moment of that dance. When I reset the needle for a third time, I sat on the edge of the sofa, convincing myself this would be the last time for the night, but I never made it back up to bed.

CHAPTER TWENTY-EIGHT

Fifteen years earlier

"Look at me," she begged as she sat half in my lap, one hand wrapped around my neck holding me in place, while two fingers from the other hand were deep inside me. I was a mirror image facing her, pleasuring her also. "I love you." She placed gentle kisses around my face.

I said nothing, even though the words begged to be released.

"It's okay," she said after a moment as she continued to move inside of me. "You don't have to say it. I know you love me." She panted as I curled my fingers. "I know it in your hands, your smile, your eyes." She rested her forehead against mine as I increased my pace. "Don't ever forget that I love you and that this means everything to me. Please remember."

When we both tipped over the edge, she felt desperate in my arms. I held her as close as she could get and whispered the world away.

Her eyes were getting heavy, but she wouldn't take them off of me. "It's getting late." I said, and instantly regretted it.

"I don't care…" She was focused on mapping out my jaw with soft touches, but I could tell she was a million miles away.

"Where are you tonight?"

"With you."

I shook my head softly, but didn't push her any further.

When the first tear hit the pillow we were sharing, I went into immediate comfort mode. I pulled her closer and kissed her temple, but the tears wouldn't stop. "Please talk to me."

"I meant what I said before."

I didn't want to acknowledge her words because then I would have to face the guilt of not releasing my own, but I wanted her out of this headspace. "I know. Please don't cry."

"I don't want to leave tonight."

"Then don't."

I held her for hours until the dawn crept in. When she left that morning, I couldn't shake the uneasy feeling that had carried over from the night before.

CHAPTER TWENTY-NINE

I leaned over the front counter of the Steam Bean. It was mid-afternoon and the students hadn't come back yet. It was a ghost town.

"Why did you leave Drew?" I asked as I played with the knobs of the espresso machine. I tried my best to appear disinterested in my own question, but it was one of the few things that seemed to constantly be front and center in my mind lately.

"I didn't. He left me." She leaned back against the counter, her arms folded, a coffee cup dangling between her fingers. "He had an affair. When I found out, he confirmed it, and then he left. He remarried shortly after."

"I'm sorry." The rumors were true after all.

"Karma."

"No." I shook my head and stopped playing with the machine. "It wasn't right when we did it and it wasn't right when he did it to you."

"It's not like we had much of a marriage at that point. We were still sleeping in the same bedroom, but we might as well have been in separate beds. We had Abbie and that was about it."

"I ran into him a couple of months after I got back." I raised my eyes for emphasis as I recalled the memory.

"That must have been fun."

"He asked me if I was going to make a play for his new wife."

She cringed. "What did you say?"

"That he knew I preferred blondes."

We both quietly chuckled.

"You're the most mature and immature person that I know all rolled into one. I've missed you," she said and took a sip from her cup.

I said nothing, not wanting to dwell on the past or any other moments that we would get stuck on.

"I was with two people my whole life, Drew and you."

Her admission was a dagger in my side, for I couldn't say the same thing.

"How many people have you been with?" she asked.

"More than two."

Her mouth twitched.

"Don't ask questions that you don't want the answers to. It will just end up hurting. Be oblivious. Pretend I'm a virgin."

"You're not a virgin now and you most certainly weren't when we were together."

"Lucky you." I offered a cheesy grin.

"Find any soul mates along the way?"

"Only stalkers."

After Lauren, there were a number of women but that all changed with Jack and the realization that I was never going to rid myself of Lauren's ghost. "We never should have happened," I said reflectively. "Who knows how your life would have turned out? Who knows how mine may have turned out? Maybe the two of you would still be together. Maybe it's time to start dating again."

"Like you?"

"Nah, you don't want to date like me. Casual isn't your style, and to be honest, I wouldn't recommend it. It can be very lonely at times. You're a wonderful person, Lauren. You could remarry again if you wanted."

"No, I meant like you and me."

"You and me?"

"*Us.*"

"There is no *us*. We can't go back."

"And you don't want to move forward. All or nothing."

"We can't go back," I said again. "We're finally at a point where we can stand to be around one another. It's a nice change."

"Only one of us had that problem."

I ignored the cheap shot. "I feel like we may actually have a friendship now, and maybe it's born completely out of our two daughters and I'm fine with that. I feel good for the first time in a really long time. It's like I'm finally doing exactly what I'm supposed to be doing. I'm exactly where I'm supposed to be."

"With Patricia?" she asked.

I shrugged. "Who knows? Maybe…" I had never given it any serious thought. Neither one of us really ever pushed the issue. A random coffee date here and a dinner there and it was enough for both of us. I knew deep down that it wasn't going anywhere, but for right now it was probably exactly what I needed.

"You're not all in with her."

"You have no idea what I am with her." I leaned forward on the counter.

"You're not all in with her," she said again. "I know what that looks like and you're not. You were all in with me."

"Well, then, she can do exactly what you did."

"What's that?"

"Whisper sweet nothings in my ear, over and over, like some sort of promise." I bit down on my tongue and briefly closed my eyes. "See?" I held up my hands, palms up, like it was the most obvious answer. Like I had just discovered sliced bread. I had trusted Lauren more than I had ever trusted anyone in my life and the fact that she had lied to me, still rattled around in the back of my mind. "There's too much history between us to take a trip down memory lane and venture into the past. It needs to stay there. We've got to move on and I've got to stop being such a petty asshole to you, otherwise, our newfound friendship is going to fall by the wayside."

"Why did you come back here?"

It was a question that I had asked myself repeatedly when I first returned. "I burned out. I worked too late. I never saw Jack. We had a nanny. The nanny got Mother's Day gifts as well as me. There's nothing wrong with that because Jack's a very considerate person…but there's a lot wrong with it. I saved enough money. I needed a change. I didn't like who I was anymore."

"But why here?"

"It was familiar and comfortable. Maybe not the best memories, but I can deal with memories. Why did you stay?"

"I fell in love with the town. Got my degree, but what do you do with a degree anymore? I kept working at the shop. The owner wanted to sell, so I bought it after the divorce."

"I need to get back to work." I tipped my cup in her direction. "To your continued good fortune." I dropped some money into the tip jar. "You'll find someone, Lauren."

"I already did."

Whether or not she meant for me to hear it, it didn't matter. I kept walking to the door.

CHAPTER THIRTY

Fifteen years earlier

When he found out, and he was always going to find out, I wasn't surprised. I wasn't shocked. A part of me wondered what had taken him so long. There was too much evidence: the after-school projects, driving me home, the sleepovers. It was all there in black and white, and all he had to do was connect the dots. When Drew found out, Lauren didn't rush over to my apartment. She didn't come and tell me in person. How could she? I received a one sentence email that only gave me more questions than answers.

He knows about us. I'll talk to you when I can.

It felt hollow and lacking, but what else was she going to say? I could only imagine what she was going through, nothing but endless questions. *How did it start? How long has it been going on? Was there anyone else? What do you mean you're bisexual?*

I didn't send an email back, because it would have been filled with my own endless questions, that began and ended with, *What happens now?* For the next week, there was nothing but silence and it made my skin crawl. She never came to the library that week and I avoided the Steam Bean at all costs. Even though I wanted to make sure she was okay, I didn't want to add anything else to her life in that moment; it felt selfish.

It wasn't until the following Monday that she showed up in class and I saw her for the first time. I half expected him to walk her to her seat, pull out her chair and proceed to punch me squarely in the face. I expected it, but it never came. When Lauren came to class that Monday, she wasn't early, nor did she come with two coffees in hand. She was right on time for the lecture. She gave me a soft nod, but her expression was completely unreadable.

Twenty minutes into the lecture, she scribbled out a note, pushed it toward me and got up from her seat and walked out of class.

I unfolded the note.

Meet me outside in two minutes.

I folded up the note and threw it into my bag. After I counted thirty seconds in my head, I couldn't wait any longer. I got up from my desk, packed up my bag and went into the hallway.

"I've missed you so much," she said as I stood in front of her. She made a move like she was going to come in for a hug, but she stopped herself and it killed me. "We can't see each other anymore." Her voice caught.

"You said…" I started and stopped. "You told me you wanted to be with me."

"I do…" If she wrung her hands together any harder, they would have cracked. "We can't anymore."

"I don't understand. This is a complete one-eighty. Did you just want to get me into bed?" I asked, but when the words left my mouth, they felt wrong, because I knew deep down that she would never do something like that to me.

"Of course not." She reached for my hands, but I pushed them away.

"We knew that this moment would come, right?"

Even if she didn't, I did. It was why I was always half-in and half-out with her, despite her promises. Why I never told her that I loved her. Why I never gave too much of myself for this very reason. We had an expiration date stamped on us the second we became involved. Unfortunately, the date had just come due. The only question that needed to be answered was what was going to happen next and that should have been the very next thing that I said, but I couldn't bring myself to do it, because I was in love with her. I thought back over the past few months, how she was initially, and who she was when she was with me. We didn't talk about their relationship, but when it came up, there was one underlying truth that I couldn't ignore.

"You aren't happy with him," I said softly.

She nodded her head but never verbalized it. "It's not that easy anymore." There was a long pause. "We have to stop."

If I wasn't looking directly at her, no one could have ever convinced me that the words that had just left her mouth belonged to her. Her voice was completely foreign. She picked him, not me, and I couldn't believe it after everything that had happened.

Instead of agreeing with her logic, I started to come undone and before I could catch myself. "You said you'd never say that to me."

There was an ache in her eyes, but she said nothing. I knew that her previous statement was just hushed words from desperate lips, but she said it and damned if I was going to let her take those words back.

"I need to try and fix this with him, especially now."

"He doesn't make you happy." It was all I could say or focus on because it was a fact. I didn't point out the obvious: I made her happy.

"I stopped trying with him."

"Is that what he told you?" I practically spit out. "You can just walk away from this? Like it's nothing?"

When she tried to wrap her arms around me, I pushed her away again.

A pained look crossed her face. "You mean *everything* to me. This is killing me."

"Don't let it. He doesn't make you happy. Let's get out of this fucking town where no one minds their business and we'll go somewhere else. Anywhere you want. Just us."

"I can't run away from this."

"No offense, but you did that months ago when you told me to kiss you everywhere and that if I missed a spot, you'd know." I paused. "Try with me."

She didn't think about it for more than a second and the words tumbled out, "Things have changed."

"What's changed?"

"I can't…"

"You can't or you won't."

"Stop being a lawyer."

"I'm not…" The air left my lungs. "Why did you want to speak to me today? Your silence for the last week spoke volumes. When you asked me to come out here, I thought you finally ended it with him and we were going to be together…" I laughed bitterly as my sanity slipped. "Message received."

She wiped furiously at her eyes.

It took everything in me not to break down. Instead, I acted out, because under no circumstance was I going to start crying. I bit down on the tremble and started to clap my hands together, slowly and loudly. The noise ricocheted off every surface in the hallway. "Goodbye, Lauren."

"What do you want me to do?"

Let's go back a week, board up the exits and remain in that moment for as long as possible. Just stay with me. But I couldn't beg. I wasn't someone who begged or pleaded. Even if I did or was capable of such an action, it wouldn't have mattered. It was clear that we didn't belong to each other. I was a day late, a dollar short, and destined to continue on without her. I kept looking for the devil, but I found her in the details and it was haunting.

"Why did you change your mind? Why did you promise me something that you never intended on keeping? What did I do wrong?"

"You didn't do anything…" When she reached for me a third time and wrapped her body around mine, it was a vice grip. She sobbed in my arms and refused to let go. "You didn't do anything," she said over and over.

I finally broke the contact because if I didn't I would have never let go. "I don't believe you. This doesn't make sense. What you're saying and how you're acting doesn't add up. So, it's got to be me." I wanted to yell. I wanted to scream. I did neither. "Something real happened between us…" I started to ramble and stopped. It didn't matter. I turned and walked away before she could reach for me again.

* * *

After she made her decision, I stopped going to class on Mondays. It was too difficult to be within a foot of her and not smile in her direction, because it would have been the wrong smile. Not look at her, because it would have been the wrong look. Undoubtedly, she would have eventually turned to me with pity in her eyes and uttered, "You have to stop."

I didn't know how to go back, so instead I plunged into the unknown without her, at least that's what I thought. She was everywhere, even though every time I looked around Renfrew, she was nowhere to be found. She flooded my dreams and my nightmares. She was random thoughts scattered throughout the hours. She was a flash of blond in a sea of people. But worst of all, she was lavender, and no matter how hard I tried, I couldn't remove the scent from my mind. How dare she. A wicked woman and me a fool.

I laid awake almost every night replaying everything. It was impossible to let go of instances where it was my decision, my words, my actions that took us further along. Everything happened too quickly, and just as quickly, it was over. When I got to the date on the calendar where we had been apart longer than we had been together, I breathed a sigh of relief and thought, today is going to be the day. I could finally take a step back and move on with my life. Time heals all wounds. That's what I had been taught, and now that time was on my side, things were going to change. I waited for the ache to ease. I waited for the weight to lift. Neither came. I simply chalked it up to the fact that it was a Monday and nothing good ever happened on a Monday, but when Tuesday came and went, a nagging nervousness settled within me. When Wednesday was looking at me with disappointment in the rearview mirror, I had a mild panic attack and came to the realization that time wasn't going to heal Lauren.

A few weeks later, our professor had an end-of-semester gathering at her house to celebrate. I didn't want to go, but I didn't know how many more opportunities I would have to see her, even if she was in the arms of her chaperone. The absence up to that point in time was too great; I needed to see her. When I walked into the party, Lauren was sitting on the end of the sofa, sans chaperone, watching the front door. I nodded in her direction and quickly walked to the punch bowl. I picked up a tea cup that was filled with a third of sweet tea and something that I couldn't place but packed a wallop. I filled up my cup again and joined her on the couch, a foot separating us. I sipped my drink and as hard as I tried, I couldn't help but get stuck on her skirt and the French stockings that covered her thighs. I sat perfectly still as the room evaporated, leaving just her and me.

She wasn't looking at me when she uttered, "Your eyes." There wasn't any hint of pity behind her words, but still I flinched.

I fixed my gaze across the room. It felt like I had been scolded. I focused on a group of students a few feet away who were animated and chatting quickly about something funny that had happened earlier in the year. I remembered that day and how the entire class erupted with laughter, but mostly I remembered how Lauren rested her head on my shoulder for the rest of class.

"You never wear skirts."

I shrugged. I pulled down the material just above my knee and crossed my legs. She was right. I never did. So why did I pick tonight of all nights to take this one out for a test drive? I knew the answer. So that she would linger on the space between my knee and a soft flowing midnight silk that matched the intensity of my feelings.

"I thought I'd change it up."

Her gaze became fixed, but I ignored it and sipped slowly from my cup trying to come up with an exit strategy. We were awkward like we had just met on some bad blind date. I half expected her phone to ring, for her to turn to me with a lame explanation of why she had to dash off. "Oh, your dog ran away with the dish *and* the spoon? How dreadful. Please don't stay a second longer." The reality that we had lost our comfortable silence that cradled me like a warm blanket was too much. I moved to get up from the couch but her hand landed on my bare knee.

"This isn't you. Do something, say something, even if it's the wrong thing," she said softly.

"We both know you don't mean that." I turned in her direction to give her an opportunity to prove me wrong, but she said nothing. I got up and headed for the door.

I was halfway down the front porch stairs when she caught up to me and reached for my elbow.

"I want to go for a walk."

"Why?"

"To talk."

"I think we've said everything we needed to say. I distinctly remember saying the only thing you wanted to hear from me a few weeks ago, *goodbye*."

"You didn't say anything!" she said and then lowered her voice. "You never say anything." She released my elbow and it looked like she was going to pull her hair in frustration.

"I shouldn't have come tonight."

"Why?"

"Because I came for the wrong reasons. I wanted to see you again. I wanted… I don't know, one more good moment between us, instead of all this." I gestured between us.

"This what?"

"This is like pulling teeth."

"Stop pretending to be someone you're not."

"What does that mean?"

"Well, the skirt for one—"

"You don't like the skirt?" I asked offended. "I specifically bought it for this moment, because I can't be myself around you."

"Yes, you can—"

"No, I can't. I don't get to be that person. You don't want me to be that person, because she would make this difficult for both of us. She would ask you a thousand questions, which you don't want to answer. She would tell you to reconsider your decision, which you don't want to hear. She would hold onto this forever and never let it go. You don't want me to really be myself. She'd make you uncomfortable. So here I am." I twirled and did a half curtsy and extended my hand. "It's nice to meet you." When she didn't take my outstretched hand, I let it fall to my side. "You act like we can just pick up where we left off, but we can't."

CHAPTER THIRTY-ONE

"*Flannel?*" I scrutinized her shirt when she sat down. A huge mistake on my part. What the hell was I doing looking at her adorable shirt anyway? I quickly deflected. "Finally decided to go from the minors to the majors, did you?"

She threw a balled-up napkin in my direction and I caught it easily.

"You're screwball still needs some work." I winked.

"Offering your services?"

But before I could answer, Betty, the town's elderly stateswoman, walked up to our table and helped herself to one of the vacant seats.

"You used to be a lawyer in the city, isn't that what I hear?"

I immediately turned to Lauren, gave her my best, *you're dead later* look and turned back to Betty. "I can't imagine who on earth would talk about me…"

Lauren slowly got out of her seat and made her way behind the counter, trying to suppress a grin.

"I was a lawyer."

"I'd like to bend your ear about a fence issue one of these days."

I cringed internally. "Betty, I no longer practice. I don't even have a license."

"All the same…" She leaned closer and whispered, "I trust you with this information."

"I thought you said it was a fence issue?"

"I'm thinking about suing my neighbor over the fence line."

"*Rita? Your best friend?*" I asked surprised because there wasn't anyone in Renfrew that hadn't lived here more than five minutes without knowing about their friendship. "You two are inseparable. Why on earth would you sue her?"

"I was talking to a realtor recently who suggested that she may have encroached on my property line."

"Oh, Betty, this is a bad idea—"

"Say I wanted to have her change the line. How would I go about doing that?"

"I would advise you not to do that."

"But if I was going to do it, how would I go about doing it?"

I wanted to pinch the bridge of my nose, but my manners held back the gesture. "If it's a small amount of money, you can go through the small claims process. You have to file some forms and appear in court, but a judge is usually able to bring the parties to an agreement."

"Where would I get those forms?"

"City Hall, but I would suggest that you think long and hard before doing that."

"Let's talk about it again when I get the forms."

"There's nothing to talk about. I'm not a lawyer anymore."

She was up and out of her seat, without even listening to the protest in my voice.

"What was that about?" Lauren asked as she sat down in Betty's vacated seat.

"You don't want to know. Why did you tell her I was a lawyer?"

"You know how she is. It's not like I had much of a choice."

"Where were we before we were rudely interrupted?"

"You couldn't keep your eyes in your head." She smirked as my eyes flashed once again to her flannel shirt and I laughed heartedly.

"*Touché*." I picked up my cup and took a long sip trying to hide my flushed cheeks.

"Maybe I should go out on a date," she blurted out, completely out of the blue.

I replayed our conversation and not once did the topic of Lauren dating come up. I looked to my right and then my left to make sure that she was in fact talking to me. When it was clear that I was the only one within ten feet of the table, I said, "Come again?"

"Dating…it's been a long time."

"You should," I said quickly and immediately regretted it.

"Any suggestions?" she asked and it felt like a trick, but I couldn't see the strings. She was a magician sawing me in half, but I didn't know where to put my legs, and she wasn't giving me any hints. Surely, they would come right off at the knees.

"*Suggestions*?" I asked dumbly, in an attempt to stall the conversation.

"For my date."

"You don't need my help. You can have—"

"Anyone I want. *Right*." Her lips wrapped around the word. "You said that once… It wasn't true then and it isn't true now, is it?"

The gargantuan elephant of resentment and repressed feelings finally had arrived. She sat in the empty chair and studied us carefully. I half expected her to take out a sketchpad.

Lauren looked at me intently, like she was challenging me. All I could do was shrug lamely, because I didn't want to get into the ins and outs of this conversation.

"There's only one person I want to date. I'd just be wasting my time…"

"You have so much to give," I argued, but she held up her hand and I shut my mouth.

"Don't. I know what I want. I know *who* I want. Just because you're terrified of your own shadow, doesn't mean that I am.

Maybe this is all we'll ever have." She gestured between the two of us. "Six months ago, I didn't even think this was possible. I never thought I'd see you again. But here you are."

"It's best to leave the past in the past."

"Are you and Patricia exclusive?"

"I don't want to talk about Patricia." I closed my eyes momentarily to ward off the headache I felt coming a mile away.

"How come? You wanted to set me up just now. I can't ask you about your girlfriend?"

"I never wanted to set you up," I said quickly. "Also, for your information, even though it's none of your business, she's not my girlfriend," I said through clenched teeth.

"Does she know that?"

"Yes, of course. We eat together sometimes."

Lauren's eyebrows practically lifted into her hairline.

"It's casual," I explained, even though I didn't owe her anything.

"Okay, let's try casual."

"I don't want to eat with you." And even though I was trying to make a joke to ease this moment, the look on her face told me that it hadn't worked.

"You won't even give it a chance?"

"I did," I paused. "Fifteen years ago."

"We're not those people anymore. I'm not going to—"

"We're enough of those people," I interjected. "Aren't we? Isn't that why you're still attracted to me? Why I'm still attracted to you?" How could I deny it after Flannel Gate? But from the look in her eyes, she wasn't expecting the admission. "I'm enjoying what we have. I don't want to complicate things between us. I like that we can get together for our kids. It's nice for them. I don't want to ruin it."

After a few moments, she said, "It hurts that it's not me."

"It's not anyone."

"Patricia…"

"It's not anyone," I said again. I swallowed down a painful lump and extended a shaky hand. "Can we just try to be friends?"

She studied my palm, which shook ever so slightly, despite my best intentions.

After a few seconds, she grasped it and held it firmly in hers.

"Friends," she mouthed back with an unfinished smile.

CHAPTER THIRTY-TWO

Fifteen years earlier

With only days left of the school year, and a week before I left this town forever, our eyes met across the quad and she suddenly stopped when she saw me. Instead of continuing on her intended path, she crossed the cobblestone and sat beside me on the bench. It was a perfect spring day filled with promise. Internally, it felt like the longest, coldest, harshest day that I had ever endured.

"I shouldn't be here," she said, and it didn't sit well with me, not after the weeks of silence.

"Then why didn't you just keep on walking by?" When I turned to her, I winced. She looked like she hadn't slept in weeks. "It's a little hot out for a sweater don't you think?

She shrugged and in the process, proceeded to wrap the material closer to her body. "I'm cold."

"That makes two of us…"

She looked out into the quad. When it didn't appear that she would do anything to stop the ever-increasing void between us, I started to ramble, which I almost never did around her. "There are words that I want to say to you, but they seem pointless now. Just a collection of letters and sounds. Less than the total of what I'm feeling. My feelings are too big for me to handle. They don't even feel like mine anymore…" I shook my head and started again. "It hurts," my voice trembled. I caught it before it fell to the ground and bruised its knees. "You are seeping into the cracks and half of me is becoming all of you. I don't want you here." I pulled at the front of my shirt. I felt desperate and the fact that I was divulging these secrets to her at this moment seemed futile.

"What do you want me to do, Kate?"

"Stay together for the kids," I muttered. I looked out to the large oak trees swaying in the warm breeze. When I looked back at Lauren she was pale.

"We don't have kids." She brushed a lock of hair behind her ear.

"It was a joke."

"A bad one."

I was perplexed by her reaction, but I let it go. "I think I'm all out of good ones. I wish I could go back to that *damn* party, no, before that…the moment when Drew placed the invitation on my desk. If I could go back to that second, I would eviscerate that piece of paper with just one look." I shook my head. "I had this feeling that night that I shouldn't go, like I would be out of place and I was right, because look at where we ended up. Look at who I've become."

"I wouldn't change anything," she whispered and I wanted to crumble.

I clenched my fist and took a deep measured breath through my nose. It felt like she had cut into me with a knife. The pain was agonizing. I wanted to keel over to try and ease the ache, but I wasn't going to give her any more ammunition.

She seemed content to sit in silence and I became absorbed in it until I looked down at the bench between us. I didn't notice it at first; I was too tired, but then the realization hit me full force. "You're not wearing your watch." It was a quiet and reflective accusation.

"No." She rubbed her wrist. "I must have forgotten it."

Wrong answer. "Isn't that just a kick in the teeth?" The realization blossomed into agitation, burrowed under my skin and started to spread.

"I don't understand."

"You're cute when you're coy, but you're not stupid. I've mentioned it enough times. I've practically begged for five more minutes, but then like clockwork, you look at your watch and you're running late and we're running out of time, and now we don't have any left." I took a deep breath that almost choked me and closed my eyes. "*Time...* It no longer exists, right? The fear of us is completely gone and you're no longer restricted by the tick, tick, tick of that damn watch." I was so painfully tired in that moment; I could have slept a thousand winters. I tried my best to swallow down the bitterness, but it still escaped. "How will you possibly know when to leave?"

She sat there stunned until she got her bearings. "I'm sure you'll tell me," she said so softly that the words almost didn't reach my ears. "I still want us to be friends..." She trailed off when I raised a single unsteady palm in the air. *Please just stop.*

"Friends?" I swallowed the bile and then the word; it felt worse than the knife, a poison in my bloodstream that would surely kill me. "*Friends?*" I asked again and then a half-scoff, half-laugh escaped my mouth. "We're *not* friends. We've never been friends. Tell me, Lauren, what does that look like to you?"

She looked down at a scuff mark on her boot. A cut in the leather from when she tripped at the library, an indelible mark. "Maybe we could get a coffee sometime? Friends get coffee." She looked up from her boots.

I realized at that moment that the mark wasn't permanent. She'd simply throw them away and buy a new pair, if not now, eventually. "Coffee?" I raised my eyebrows. "Is that what you want from me? *Coffee?* I don't need your fucking pity coffee."

"Kate, you don't understand... I'm—"

"Don't." My shoulders sagged and my breath caught. "I got in." The words slipped out, despite my intention not to tell her.

"You got in?"

"Law school."

There was a long pause before she spoke again. "Here?" she asked, and I couldn't fathom why there was hope in her voice.

I shook my head.

"Are you leaving?"

"I haven't decided yet." It was a lie, but what did it matter? I got up from the bench and walked away into the insufferable cold. I never looked back.

CHAPTER THIRTY-THREE

I picked up two handfuls of wet snow and packed them together until they formed a tight ball. I hurled it at the Steam Bean's front window and it hit with a loud bang, busting apart and streaming down the window in icy chunks. Before I could stop myself or even question what the hell I was doing, I picked up another handful and threw it at the storefront and an even bigger bang rang out.

Lauren came running out in her blue apron and white long-sleeve shirt. She stopped when she realized that I was the thirteen-year-old asshole that she was about to reprimand.

I picked up another handful and started to form the wet snow between my hands.

"Are you insane?" she asked, hands on her hips. She was breathless and irritated and it was the most beautiful she'd ever looked.

"Certifiable. Want to see the paperwork?" I smiled and aimed the snowball in her direction.

"You wouldn't," she challenged as she reached for her own handful of snow.

I edged closer, ever watchful of her hands, trying to anticipate her next move. "No? Pretty sure I would."

"Are you flirting with me?" she asked as she kept an eye on my arm and the other on her own snowball.

I laughed loudly. "With you?" I hurled the snow in her direction and she dodged it easily. "That seems rather pointless, doesn't it?"

She came within ten feet of me and drew her hand back. I held out my arms and gave her a clear target of my chest. She held her hand up for a second and then her arm dropped to her side. "It's not fun if you don't run... You're just a sitting duck."

"I'm tired of running. Tired of chasing." I emphasized the target on my chest. "Hit me. It's only fair. I got the shop twice. Take your best shot."

She hesitated for a second and then dropped the snowball to the ground.

My face fell. "Just what I thought." I shook my head and lowered my arms. I released a sigh and walked past her. "Same old Lauren," I muttered.

She grabbed me by the arm. "What the hell does that mean?"

I faced her. "You were only ever interested in the game, and when it got serious, you lost interest."

Her grip on my arm tightened. "Is that what you think happened? You and I aren't a game."

"You acted like we were," I said, even though I knew it wasn't true. I shrugged out of her grasp.

I was a few feet down the road when a wet snowball his me square in the back. The sensation shocked me and I stopped. When I turned around, another one hit me on the top of my right shoulder. I blinked at Lauren as she gathered more snow and walked toward me. I held out my arms, giving her another target, but she just kept coming closer. "This doesn't have to be difficult," she said gently as she held the snow loosely in her hands.

"What?" I asked.

"*Us.*"

"There is no—"

She mushed the snow into my face, the cool wetness was like an ice bath trickling into my coat and dripping down into my shirt.

"There's *always* been an *us*," she punctuated each word. "There will *always* be an *us*. The sooner you accept it, the better off you'll be." She turned on her heel and was back in the coffee shop as the snow trailed down my face, a smile edging out just past my lips.

CHAPTER THIRTY-FOUR

Jack jumped into bed and snuggled into me.

"Morning, Mom," she said in a sleepy voice.

"Morning." I brushed back the hair from her face. "Good sleep?"

"Uh-huh. Can we work on my Valentine's Day cards for the class this weekend?"

"Of course, we should go to the store today and get some."

"Mom?"

"Yeah?"

"How do you know when you love someone?"

I squinted down at my daughter. *Damn it.* I knew that this conversation began and ended with a certain other ten-year-old. "You just know, kiddo."

"But how?"

"Well, there are a lot of ways to tell, but generally when you care about someone's happiness more than your own, that's a pretty good sign."

"Like how?"

I thought about it for a moment. "When you're willing to give up your dessert to make the other person happy, you probably love them."

"I think I'd give my dessert to Abbie."

And there it was.

"She'd probably let me have a bite," she rambled on.

"I'm sure Abbie would share with you. She's very considerate."

Jack nodded happily. "She is."

I closed my eyes. I wanted out of this conversation.

"Mom?"

"Yeah?"

"You wouldn't share your dessert with Patricia the other night."

"She picked fruit, she gets fruit," I chuckled softly. "I only share my dessert with you."

"Wouldn't it be nice to share it with someone else?"

I pulled her close and planted a firm kiss to the top of her head. "Then you won't get any of my desserts."

She sat quietly beside me for a moment, until she looked up at me. "You shared your cupcake with Ms. Dawson at Christmas."

I blinked, went to speak and stopped. "That's because you and Abbie ate all of the cupcakes." I tickled her sides until she squirmed.

"We left two cupcakes, Mom…"

It was like she was doing math, but no one had asked her to solve this particular problem. I sighed, pulled her close and planted another kiss on her head.

* * *

Lauren leaned over my desk, with a shirt that had one too many buttons undone for my liking. It's not that I didn't like it. I liked it very much and she knew it. The twinkle in her eye as she caught my gaze roaming from time to time told me as much. I forced my eyes to remain on hers as she asked her next question.

"Do you want to come to an aloe vera party on Valentine's Day?"

"*A what?*" I asked dumbly. Why the hell were we talking about aloe vera?

She picked up my library stamp and a loose sheet of paper and started to stamp out patterns on the paper. "Someone comes to teach you about organic beauty products and how to properly put on makeup…" She trailed off, no doubt, after looking at my shocked expression. "All of my single friends are coming. I'm going to have some appetizers and wine, share some stories." She asked with a hopeful look, but that hope quickly turned to doubt as my expression continued.

"So, it's Jamestown with eyeliner?"

She laughed but said nothing.

"Are you kidding me? Please tell me that you're joking."

"Nope. I got dragged into it. I'm hosting…" She picked up my pen and started to scribble hearts on the paper; it was just like college all over again.

I stilled her hand because she was already the most distracting woman that I had ever met in my life. I didn't need the added bonus of her playing with all of my stationery. "Look, only if Jack's life depended on it would I ever attend something like that, and between you and me, it's a *big* if."

"It's going to be all women," she said, trying to get my attention.

"As if you'd let me speak to any of them long enough to strike up a half-decent conversation."

"I don't know what you're talking about."

"Morgan," I coughed loudly. "*Morgan,*" I said again.

She raised one eyebrow in response. "She was drunk."

"Right-hand side of the room, fourth row, second seat."

"Who?" A confused look crossed her face.

"A woman that I pointed out to you on our first day of Women's Literature. You told me that I could do better."

She smiled at the memory. "You did." She pointed at herself.

I shook my head as I tried to pry the stationery from her hands, but she swatted me away and continued with her hearts.

"It's probably going to be all straight women," I muttered more to myself, because we both knew that I would be at the party.

"You can bring Patricia if you want," she said slowly as she focused intently on the page in front of her.

"No," I said quickly.

"You don't want to spend Valentine's Day with her?"

"No comment."

"I'll be there," she said even quicker.

"Yes, the token bisexual, of course." I winked playfully and grabbed my own pen and started to fill up Lauren's sheet with stars.

"Jack's coming."

"My daughter wants to attend a makeup party?" I blinked away the confusion. "I don't recall her ever asking for my permission to attend such an event. Jack and I are going to have a long conversation about going above and beyond for girls that she has crushes on." I shook my head. "Jack would do anything for Abbie."

"You wouldn't do anything for me? What if I begged, Kate? If I remember correctly, you used to love when I begged you."

I quickly sat back in my chair as my ears roared, and looked around the library. It was late in the afternoon, and thankfully most of the students were in class. I drew an imaginary line across the desk between us. "You're getting very close to crossing the friendship line, Ms. Dawson."

"You'll live. Please?"

"You're wasting your breath."

But we both knew that she wasn't, so why was she even bothering me with this anymore? She should have just taken my phone, punched the date and time into my calendar and been done with it, but then the back and forth, the banter, the time together wouldn't have been possible. So much of my relationship with Lauren lived and breathed in those moments. It's what made us who we were and it's what made walking away from her so utterly unbearable.

She picked up a fresh sheet of paper and scribbled something with my pen. She folded it in half and placed it in the middle of my desk, exactly where I had drawn the imaginary line. She leaned back in her chair, looked at the sheet, and looked at me.

I leaned back in my own chair, put my feet up on the desk, looked at the note and smiled. So, she wanted to play a game. That was just fine with me, even if I was at work. "Something you want to tell me, sweetheart?" I almost choked on the word, but I got it out. If she wanted to play with me and presumably my emotions, I could do the same thing.

Her gaze locked onto mine.

"It's in the note."

I dropped my feet from the desk and pulled out a fresh sheet of paper. I scribbled out words that I had pushed from my mind for years. In a matter of moments, they were pouring out onto the page. I had nearly filled up half the sheet and then looked down at my work. I re-read it and shook my head. I placed the cap back on my pen, folded up the paper, ripped it in half, in quarters, and tossed the shreds into the garbage bin.

"Didn't like what you wrote?" she asked after a couple of moments.

"I'm not that person anymore."

"Yes, you are." She pushed her note across the imaginary line, until it was laying right in front of me.

I didn't move to reach for it. I didn't do anything. Whatever it said could remain hidden for the rest of eternity. I didn't need anything else to put in a box under my bed.

She pointed down at the note with her index finger. "I'm still this person. Read it, rip it up, or do nothing." She tapped on the note and turned to leave. "I'll see you at the party."

I watched her push through the doors and out of the library. I looked down at the note. I didn't want to open it. But...I had to know. I took a deep breath and unfolded the note and laid it flat on my desk.

Kate,

i miss you.

i miss you when you're sitting right across from me. How is that possible?

Do you ever miss me?

Lauren.

I clutched my sides. I quickly swiped the note from my desk and threw it into my top drawer. I grabbed my coat and headed for the exit. I needed air. I needed to get out of the library and away from my desk. When I pushed through the doors, Lauren was on the other side, leaning against the building. She was surprised to see me, but I didn't pay her any attention. I walked right past her, desperate to get air into my lungs so that I could breathe again.

* * *

As soon as Jack ran into the house, Lauren pulled me in by my shirt. "Everyone, this is Kate, she has generously volunteered to be the canvas for tonight."

"What? *No.*" I tried to push away her hands as I whispered harshly, in a half-panic.

"Mom, really?" Jack asked, both surprised and excited.

I glared at Lauren. "I'm going to kill you…slowly. Something with spiders. Then I'm going to revoke your library privileges come Monday morning. Thankfully, a new generation of Sapphic readers will finally be able to access our collection… since they all seem to be permanently checked out to a Ms. Dawson."

"Won't I already be dead?" She grinned.

"Nope, that's how slow it's going to be."

"Hi, Kate. I'm Pam." The makeup artist introduced herself. It was so bright, so cheery, that it had to be fake, but the longer I stared at her, I realized that it wasn't.

I turned back to Lauren. "Spiders that lay eggs."

"Ewww!" Pam exclaimed. "No more of that kind of talk for the rest of the night. Let's have a fun girl's night and learn about makeup."

"Pam, this really isn't my thing. Anyone else would be much better suited for this."

But it was too late as she was already pushing me into a chair and all of Lauren's single friends had gathered round. "Look at this skin." She ran her fingertips over my cheek and I flinched.

The rest of the evening went by in a blur and no matter how hard I tried to squirm out of that chair, three pairs of eyes kept me seated.

Lauren walked back into the living room and handed me a wipe after her guests and the dreaded Pam had finally left for the evening.

"No comments?" I asked as I started to peel the makeup off my face.

"You are always stunning, but this isn't you. The kids liked it, though."

"Well, as long as the kids liked it…" I grumbled, but it was half-hearted. I enjoyed seeing their reactions, as well as Lauren's.

"Did you have a good time?"

"No," I said with a smile.

"Liar."

"I would have had a better time if someone would have given me two seconds of breathing room to get Stacey's number."

"I have no idea what you're talking about." She took the wipe from my hand. "You missed some spots." She brought her fingers under my chin and tilted my head in her direction. I instinctively closed my eyes, because it was impossible to be that close and not get completely lost in her. I remained stock still as she gently removed the final traces. "Besides," she said quietly, "I was protecting Patricia's honor."

That caused me to open my eyes and I rolled them dramatically. "Patricia and I keep each other company. It's nothing more than that."

She hummed as she removed the last of the makeup, but she didn't remove her fingers, and I didn't close my eyes.

"Did you ever stop and think about how much you and I keep each other company?"

I thought about it often. I looked deep into her eyes and tried with all of my might to be convincing. "No," I said softly, but it was another lie and she knew it.

CHAPTER THIRTY-FIVE

As Jack and I waited on the porch for the pizza to arrive, Lauren pulled into the driveway with Abbie and her sleepover bag in tow. I smiled at both of them as Jack raced to grab Abbie's bag. Lauren slowly walked up the steps, looking intently at me, and I was putty. How, after all this time, could the mere sight of her lighten up everything in my being?

"Would you like to come in? I just ordered pizza for the girls and there's more than enough for you to have some as well," I said to Lauren, my hands now on Jack's shoulders as she quickly chatted with Abbie.

"Mom has a date tonight," Abbie blurted and went back to talking to Jack.

I remained perfectly still. "Oh."

"It's not a date." Lauren shook her head and gave me a quick reassuring smile.

Abbie tilted her head to the side. "Mr. Abraham said it was a date."

"Honey, someone saying, 'it's a date,' doesn't necessarily make it so."

"So, you do have a date," I managed to get out. "That's nice. Mr. Abraham, is it?" I asked as I tried to run through every damn citizen in this town to place him. "Does he have a first name?" I looked down at Abbie, hopeful that another tidbit or two would come rolling out of her mouth.

"Barry," Lauren said deliberately. When I looked up, her eyes sparkled. "Are you jealous?" She bit down on her lower lip.

"*Pfft...*" I tried to sound indignant, but I sounded like a thirteen-year-old going through puberty. "Of Barry Abraham? *Please...*" I held tightly onto Jack's shoulders.

"Mom? Can I go inside with Abbie?"

"Of course." I gave her a strange look.

"You won't let go."

"Right..." I swallowed and released my daughter. "Pizza should be here soon," I called out to the two retreating figures, as I completely ignored Lauren and her smug look.

I dug my hands into my pockets. "So, how long have you known Barry?"

"Almost ten years."

I took my hands out of my pockets and clasped them together awkwardly. "Wonderful," I said as I rocked back and forth on my heels.

"It's incredible."

"That's great for you guys," I swallowed nauseously.

"No." She studied me. "You're completely freaking out right now. Do you know that? Barry is the shop's bookkeeper. He's in his seventies."

"Oh..." I spluttered and puberty was back. "A May to December romance, how very twenty-first century of you." I tried to joke but it fell flat.

"Did you really think I had a date?"

I raised my hands in the air as I did everything that I could to wall up my emotions. "Abbie said..." I put my hands back in my pockets and planted my feet. I took a deep breath. "You should date, even if he is seventy." At least this time I got a little smile.

"Don't start that again. It's like a broken record and I'm starting to get tired of hearing it."

CHAPTER THIRTY-SIX

I blinked in disbelief. "Does this area really need to be mopped right now?" I asked Lauren, as I turned my attention from Patricia. "Furthermore, don't you have underlings to do this?"

"Yes, it does. Don't let me interrupt you." She pointed between Patricia and me.

My eyes widened and I gave her a knowing look.

"I was thinking that maybe we could go away this weekend," Patricia said as she ignored my wandering gaze.

"You have the girls this weekend," Lauren spoke softly as she looked at me.

I felt like asking her if she wanted to pull up a chair, but I was ninety-nine percent sure that she would have taken me up on my offer.

Patricia looked at Lauren and then back to me. "Girls?"

"Our daughters are best friends. The sleepovers alternate on most weekends. Kate has them this weekend," Lauren offered, although no one had asked her directly.

"Oh, okay." Patricia turned back to me. "Next weekend then?"

"Let me look at a calendar and I will call you tonight."

"Great. I have to get going. I have a class in fifteen minutes." She squeezed my hand resting on the top of the table. "Call me."

Lauren sat down in Patricia's vacant seat before the door swung closed.

"Finished your mopping?" My voice dripped with sarcasm.

"Yep."

"That was *really* mature." I shook my head, disapprovingly.

"So is coming into *my* coffee shop and planning future dates. Real mature."

"Believe me, I didn't pick the location." I wouldn't have done that to myself or Lauren voluntarily.

"Going away for the weekend... I guess it's safe to say you're girlfriends now." She prodded and pried.

"Don't," I said quickly.

"Why can't I ask that?"

"You can ask it, but I don't have to answer."

Betty chose that moment to knock loudly on the windowpane, and although I was grateful for the distraction, I groaned when she waved a set of forms excitedly.

"Fuck me," I muttered.

"Uh oh." Lauren looked out to Betty

"This is all your doing."

"What does she want?"

"Like you don't know."

"I don't. She asked if you still practiced."

"Betty wants to sue Rita over an inch of fence on her property line."

"Are you representing her?"

"God no. I told her that I would help her with the forms."

"Rita is going to be *so* mad at you." Lauren laughed as she walked away and Betty sat down.

"Kate, I got the forms."

"Betty, this is a bad idea. If I was your lawyer—"

"You are my lawyer."

"No," I said firmly. "I don't practice anymore, so I can't be your lawyer. But if I was, I would strongly advise against this. It's an inch of property, *an inch*. How many years have you known Rita?"

"Thirty-five," Betty said proudly.

"Thirty-five years," I repeated. "Are you willing to throw away thirty-five years of friendship over one inch? Because that's what you're going to do. This is going to take up a lot of your time and money. These types of issues, *fence issues*, you're better off going to the bank, taking out a pile of money and lighting it on fire in your backyard. At least there would be some excitement in that. I bet the whole town would come to watch. Fence claims are like lighting money on fire, but this one is worse because Rita will never forgive you." I paused and sighed. "If you can live with that, and you still want me to show you how to do the forms, I will."

"You don't think she would ever forgive me?"

"I can almost guarantee it. Besides, it's not like Rita did this intentionally. When the fence went up, it would have been the contractor who messed up the line. Rita had nothing to do with it. Do you honestly think she would have told him, 'Make sure you take an extra inch from Betty because I want to take advantage of her good nature?'"

"Rita wouldn't do that," she said quickly.

"Exactly. Your feelings are valid, but at the end of the day, is it really worth just one inch? Neither one of you are moving anytime soon. The next time the fence needs to be replaced, just remind Rita and the contractor of the line."

"When you say it like that, it isn't worth ruining our friendship over an inch."

"Thank God," I muttered.

"How much do I owe you for your time?"

"You don't owe me anything."

"Thanks for the legal advice."

"It wasn't legal advice."

"I know, I know, you're not a lawyer." She used air quotes and it amused me. "You're a librarian. I'll bake you something and bring it over to the library." She got up, threw the forms in the trash, and left.

I sat back in my chair and sighed heavily, not because of what had happened with Betty, but because of what had happened with Patricia and Lauren five minutes beforehand. Was it getting serious with Patricia? Is that what I wanted to happen? Patricia was sweet and kind, but... She wasn't Lauren, and I knew what I had do next.

* * *

There was a knock at the front door and it startled Jack momentarily. It would have startled me too given the hour, but I was expecting it. "It's Patricia." I turned to Jack. "Can you get up to bed? I'll be up there in a couple of minutes."

"Why is she here so late?"

"I needed to talk to her quickly. Get started on your teeth. I won't be longer than twenty minutes and then you and I can read the next chapter, okay?"

"I'm going to time you."

"I know you will."

As she ran up the stairs, I made my way to the front door and motioned Patricia into the living room. "Can I get you something to drink?" I offered as she sat down on the sofa.

"Will I need a drink? Your message sounded a bit serious."

I expelled a breath, not because I was nervous, but because I had put myself in this position in the first place. "I don't think we should see each other any longer."

She studied me for a few seconds before she spoke. "I'd like to say that I'm surprised, but I'm not... I was hoping you'd come around."

"You're a wonderful woman–"

"*Kate*, I'm going to stop you right there. Please don't tell me about how wonderful I am while you're breaking up with me; it's insulting."

"I'm sorry. You've been very patient with me and I've been wasting your time."

"Then don't waste it."

"I have feelings for someone else and no matter what I do…" I sighed deeply. "I just can't seem to get over them."

"Lauren?"

I said nothing.

"It's obviously Lauren," she said again like she needed the confirmation.

"Nothing has happened with her, but nothing is going to happen between us either. I'm sorry."

"*Something* has happened with Lauren."

"We were involved in college for a very brief period of time. I didn't come back here for her, but here she was, and the past just won't stay buried. I had thought…" Another sigh escaped my lips. "I had tried for many years to get over what happened, but it's clear that I haven't and maybe I never will."

"Does she still have feelings for you?"

"Yes, but it doesn't matter."

"Why not?"

"She and I are…" I made a little explosion gesture with my hands. "Explosive. There's no in-between, and there never has been."

"Sounds intense."

"I can't imagine you want to talk about this."

"I don't. I would like to continue our friendship if that's possible."

"I'd like that."

She got up from the couch and headed toward the door. "Good luck with Lauren."

I sat on the couch and shook my head. There was no luck when it came to Lauren.

CHAPTER THIRTY-SEVEN

I walked into the Steam Bean with a smile on my face; it faltered only slightly the moment that I couldn't find Lauren. I scanned the small confines of the shop at least a dozen times looking for a flash of blond as I waited in line, but to no avail. Where was she?

"What can I get you, Kate?" the barista asked, pulling me from my thoughts.

I knew at that moment that I had become predictable. Someone who I had never spoken with before recognized me and knew my name because I was considered a regular. It was time to seriously rethink instant coffee in the mornings. I moved forward to the cash register. "Is Lauren in the back?" I asked, even though I didn't want to. I wanted her to magically appear and we could have our normal morning routine like we always did, and then perhaps I wouldn't look so obvious.

"She came down with something this morning and left a couple of hours ago."

"She's sick?"

"Just a cold. Can I get you a large chocolate-vanilla latte?"

I was completely taken back. "She's not the barista today." I was on the verge of pointing an accusatory finger in his direction.

"I won't tell." He winked and started to punch in the order.

I felt personally attacked. How many other employees knew what I was and wasn't allowed to order depending on who was behind the counter? My mind swirled. Had she talked to them about me when I wasn't there? Or had they simply taken notice over time? This went beyond being considered a regular.

"No…" I looked at him like he was a few coupons short of a free toaster, but I was the one that felt less than whole and I didn't know why. "Just a regular coffee to go."

An hour later, when I climbed the steps to the two-story craftsman, I came armed with supplies. I knocked my customary three times, and just when I was about to knock again, the door finally opened revealing Lauren in sweats. She looked white as a ghost with a Kleenex covering her mouth.

"What are you doing out of bed?" I asked, like she was being completely ridiculous for answering the door.

She tried to roll her eyes, but I could tell she didn't have the strength.

I didn't wait for an invitation. I crossed the threshold and ushered her back inside. She walked slowly into the living room, her arms wrapped around her body, and headed straight for the couch, which she had turned into a cocoon of blankets and pillows.

I put my bag of supplies down on the coffee table and started to pull the items out one by one.

"I already have Kleenex," she sniffled.

"No, you have two-ply. This is three sheets with lotion in the layers. Your nose won't get raw." I discarded the top and pulled one out and passed it to her.

She held it up against her cheek. "*Oh*," came the stuffy reply.

"I know."

She leaned back against the sofa with her bare feet tucked underneath her.

"Why the hell don't you have socks on?"

"It took too much effort." She buried her face into the pillows and tried to cover her feet haphazardly with the blankets which looked like a whole lot more effort than just getting a pair of socks in the first place.

"You were able to get all of your bedding from upstairs and you couldn't grab a pair of socks? You need to stay warm." I pointed to her feet. "Heat loss."

I sat down on the coffee table opposite the couch and pulled out a container of Vicks and a thick pair of winter socks. She looked up just as I was unscrewing the lid.

"I hate Vicks," she whined.

"*I hate Vicks*," I mimicked back like a small child as I put down the container and reached for her ankles.

"What are you doing?" she asked but didn't pull away when I put her feet in my lap.

Her feet were like ice. I sighed loudly as I rubbed them between my hands, trying to warm them up. "You'll thank me later." I scooped up some of the ointment onto a tissue and rubbed it into her right foot. When I'd finished with both feet and put the winter socks on, I said, "There, don't take those off. When it stops tingling apply some more and make sure you put on some before bed."

She tucked her feet back under the covers and laid down facing me. "Where did you learn that?"

"My grandmother. There's some chicken stew from my freezer in there." I pointed to the bag. "Enough for lunch and dinner. You need to eat and drink fluids." I pulled out two small pill bottles and handed her the capsules. "Take two every four hours."

"What are they?"

"Different herbs to boost your immune system."

"Why are you being so nice to me?"

I stopped my rummaging and looked back at her. "I don't want you to die," I deadpanned. "Drew would never let me see Abbie." I winked and it was the first half-smile she'd offered. "Speaking of Abbie, I'm going to bring her to my house for dinner. If you're feeling better, I'll bring her home, but if it's worse, she'll stay with us for the night. No arguments."

She settled for a moment with her eyes closed and I thought she may fall asleep, but then she leaned up suddenly. "How did you know I was sick?"

"You weren't at the Steam Bean."

"Did you order it without me?" She eyed me suspiciously, which was adorable given her current state.

I shook my head.

She nodded to herself as her eyes started to glaze over. "That's an *us* thing," she said nonsensically as she put her head back down on her pillow and closed her eyes.

I put my palms down on the coffee table to brace myself for my next admission. "I know it is."

Her eyes opened. "I love you."

"Shhh…" My fingertips pressed firmly into the woodgrain. "You're sick and you're not feeling well. You're saying things that if you didn't have a bunch of medication in your system and a head cold, you wouldn't be saying. Close your eyes, go to sleep. I'll stay for a bit and if you need anything, I'm right here."

She looked at me with her last ounce of energy, like she wanted to put up a fight, but couldn't muster anything else. "I love you."

"I know."

She sighed and closed her eyes.

I watched as her breathing became shallow and the first tendrils of sleep pulled her under. I moved from my perch on the coffee table into the armchair. Softer than a church mouse I whispered, "I love you too." I released the words after fifteen years so that they wouldn't be stuck in my head on repeat like some love song that I was trying to sink into my soul.

CHAPTER THIRTY-EIGHT

When I was paged over the loudspeaker at work, I immediately knew something was wrong. It was the first time in my history of working at the library that it had ever happened. When I got to the front desk, Lauren was on the phone. Jack was in the hospital. I froze and her words wouldn't register. I drove my car as fast as I could, raced across the parking lot and burst through the emergency room doors. Lauren and Abbie sat off to the side in a busy waiting room. Abbie was the first one to look up, and when she did, she ran toward me, threw her arms around my hips and started to cry. "I told her not to go up into the tree. I told her!" she sobbed into my hip.

I looked over to Lauren, panic coursing through my body. She stood and approached me with reassuring hands. "It's okay, Kate," she said slowly and deliberately as she stroked Abbie's hair, trying to soothe her, but it soothed me all the same. "The girls were playing and Jack fell. She needs a couple of stitches. We would have stayed with her, but they said it was family only."

I shook my head in complete and utter disbelief at the most asinine policy I had ever heard of in my life. *They left my daughter alone in the emergency room.* I wanted to scream. I would destroy this fucking hospital.

"It's okay, honey." I squeezed Abbie's shoulder. "I'm not mad," I said gently, but she continued to cry into my hip. "Shhh... I'm not mad. Let me go and see how Jack's doing, okay?"

I walked over to the Plexiglas window and peered in at a woman dressed in light blue scrubs. I took my license out of my wallet and placed in on the counter. "I'm Kate Connors. My daughter Jacquelyn Connors was admitted."

She glanced quickly at my identification and buzzed me in. "She's in bed six." She pointed down the long corridor, but before I even took a step down the hall, I glared at her. "How dare you leave my daughter alone in the emergency room." I said, ready to attack, my incisors on full display.

"Ma'am that's hospital pol–"

"You better *pray* that the only injuries that she has are the ones that she came in with or I will slap a medical malpractice suit on this hospital so fast your head will spin, and I'll name you as a defendant personally for leaving her unattended."

I stormed down the hall until I reached Jack's bed. She sat at the end with her legs dangling in the air. "Mom! I need stitches," she said excitedly.

"You're going to need a lot more than that by the time I'm done," I said sternly and then counted to five in my head to push the anger back down. *She was okay.* I exhaled deeply as I closed the distance between us. *She was going to be okay.* I pushed the air through my body.

"I'm sorry." The excitement was completely gone from her voice.

I gently took her head in my hands and tilted it backward. Just above her right eye was a bloody square of gauze. When I peeled it back, there was a small gash. "Jesus, Jack, what the hell were you thinking?"

"I wanted to get Abbie a cherry blossom."

"From where?" I started to run my fingers over the back of her head in search of cuts and bumps.

"The tree in their backyard."

"Jack, you can reach up and grab one."

"The nicest ones were at the top," she whispered.

"That's a twenty-foot drop. Are you insane?" My eyes widened in disbelief. "You could have broken a bone or something much worse. You put Ms. Dawson in an awful position by doing this." I tried to count to ten, but I only made it to three, when I cried, "You cannot climb up the highest tree to impress a girl you like!" I said it louder than I wanted, but I needed to make this point abundantly clear.

"You would," she shot back.

"Are you kidding me? You're in no position to mouth back right now. You're grounded. No sleepover with Abbie this weekend."

"Mom!"

"Not another word or the next one is cancelled too."

"Mom, you would have done it too." She was on the verge of tears but held them back.

"You know what, Jack? You're right. I probably would have done it too, but I would have been damn sure that I didn't fall. What would have happened if you would have fallen on Abbie and hurt her?"

She quickly released the argument that was on the tip of her tongue. "That would've been awful…"

"You think?"

At that moment, the emergency room doctor graced us with his presence, releasing some of the tension in the room. He extended his hand. "Ms. Connors, I'm Jack's doctor. It's nice to meet you. Jack's had quite the adventure today," he said, a little too happily for my liking. The scowl I leveled in his direction took some of the pep out of his step and he cleared his throat. "Other than the laceration, she's going to be fine. I'm thinking two stitches should be enough to close the wound. We have no concern that she sustained a concussion. There are no contusions or gaps in her memory. Keep an eye on her for the next couple of days, and if anything changes, come back immediately."

After another hour of waiting for Jack to be stitched up, we finally exited back into the waiting room, where a tired looking Lauren and Abbie were still seated.

"You didn't have to wait." I gave Lauren a sympathetic look.

"Of course, we were going to wait."

Jack's eyes lit up when she saw Abbie. "I got two stitches," she said, pointing to the new patch of gauze just above her eye.

Abbie ran up to Jack and threw her arms around her in a tight hug. "That was stupid," she said loudly into Jack's ear, and I nodded my head enthusiastically.

"I know, I know…" Jack crossed her arms, clearly exhausted by all of the women in her life telling her that she was wrong. "I can't come over this weekend," she said to Abbie with her head down, sighing heavily into the waiting room. It felt like we were on the verge of our second emergency of the day.

"*What*!" Abbie shrieked. "Why?" She immediately turned to me with tears in her eyes.

"Jack's grounded for this weekend." I put my hand on Jack's shoulder.

"We're sorry," Abbie whined and her tears started to fall.

"Thanks a lot, Kate." Lauren's head tilted up to the ceiling, clearly exasperated by the events of the day and what was to come. I couldn't blame her. For the last few hours, she had dealt with the panic and fear of Jack falling, getting her to the hospital, and waiting for me to arrive. This whole day, coupled with Abbie's current devastation was in all likelihood putting her on the precipice of a migraine or at the very least a splitting headache.

I offered the most sympathetic look that I could muster at the moment and mouthed, *I'm sorry*.

Jack grabbed Abbie's hand and they walked toward the exit. As Lauren and I trailed behind them, I could hear Jack whisper, "It's okay. Shhh… You can still come over next weekend if we're good. Mom swore that we could still see each other next weekend." It was the only promise that I could make to prevent dealing with an inconsolable Jack.

"Don't you think they've been through enough?" Lauren asked, as we walked ten paces behind them.

"She could have seriously hurt herself or Abbie." I shook my head in disbelief. "Sorry for being the adult that no one likes." I paused as we continued down the well-worn corridor. "Thank you for getting her to the hospital. I'm sorry she did this."

"It's okay," she sighed. "She's okay. That's all that matters."

There was a chill to the early evening air when we left the hospital and made our way through the parking lot. Lauren wrapped her arms around her chest, hugging her body. I wanted to wrap her in something to ward off the cold, but my arms seemed completely inappropriate at that moment.

As I neared our car, I called out to Jack. "Come on Jack, say goodbye."

She quickly hugged Abbie who was still visibly and audibly upset. "I'll see you on Monday." Jack put her hands on Abbie's shoulders like she was swearing fealty.

"Okay..." A small hiccup escaped as Abbie wiped at her eyes.

Even though none of this was my fault and I was only trying to be a good parent, the romance novels would not be kind in their depiction of me when Jack and Abbie's great romance was penned. I imagine that I would be reduced to a second cousin, twice removed, of the Capulet family. I offered one more sympathetic look to Lauren. "Good night."

"Don't be too hard on her, Kate. You would have done it too." She gave me a knowing look.

I muttered my disagreement, got into the car, and started the engine. A couple of seconds later, Jack climbed into the front passenger seat. I turned to her. "You know what we're going to do this weekend?"

"What?"

"Discuss why you don't do stupid things for girls."

"Mom," she said with an exasperated tone. "I know."

"Clearly you don't!" I half-yelled and then tried to calm myself with the mantra, she's all right, she's all right, she's all right. I expelled a deep breath that I didn't realize I had been holding until it started to choke me. "Summertime is almost here. What if you would've broken your leg? Who would have ridden bikes with Abbie?"

She had nothing to say but shifted in her seat.

"I betcha someone else would have done that stuff with Abbie, not you. You don't put yourself in a position where you can't spend time with her, does that make sense?"

"Yes," she said slowly as the wheels in her head started to turn. "That's a good tip."

"Yeah, a good tip…" I pulled out of the parking lot.

The phone rang a couple of hours later and Lauren's number flashed across the screen. I picked it up and said nothing as I waited for the pleading little voice of a ten-year-old, begging me to reconsider my punishment.

When no little voice pushed through the silence, I finally said, "Hello?"

"You're not very popular at my house this evening," Lauren teased.

I wanted to come back with a witty retort, something along the lines of, "When was I ever popular at your house?" Instead, I sighed into the phone. "Lauren…"

Of course, Abbie would get Lauren to call. She was a diabolical mastermind, or at least that's what I believed to be absolutely certain at that moment. She was ten and had only known me for a brief period of time, but she had already discovered my Achilles' heel. I brought my fingers to the bridge of my nose and pinched slightly. "Abbie can't talk to Jack right now. She's grounded."

"I know, that's not why I'm calling," she said and then she took a sip of something and I was instantly mesmerized.

Water? Wine? The options played over in my mind. I settled on whiskey. I looked over to the cabinet where a half-full decanter sat, and I pushed away the memories. "Sorry. Why are you calling?"

Another long drawn out sip like she was giving herself additional time. It was like she hadn't thought through exactly what she wanted to talk about, which wasn't Lauren. She always knew what she wanted to say. "I was supposed to talk to you about something today, but then Jack fell and we didn't have time." She paused and took another sip.

A million different scenarios raced through my mind. *Talk? About what?* A nervous energy bubbled up inside of me.

"The girls want to go camping," she uttered, effectively short-circuiting my thoughts.

"After today? Are you kidding me?"

"No one was seriously hurt," she said in a soothing tone and sipped again. If this was anyone else, the sipping would have irritated me and I would have hung up the second time it happened, but it was the only thing that I was really focused on. "They asked me to speak to you before all of this happened."

"Maybe they need to spend some time apart. This is ridiculous."

"No," Lauren said quickly and there was a quiet thud. I assumed that she put her tumbler down.

"Excuse me?"

"I've already dealt with a crying, sulking ten-year-old for the last two hours since you told Abbie that Jack wasn't coming over. I can't even imagine how wonderful she'll be tomorrow. So, *no*, that's not happening."

I knew from her tone that the conversation was effectively over and the decision had already been made. "When did we start co-parenting these children?" I said under my breath, not really wanting or needing her answer. "One adult and two kids on a camping trip, that's a lot."

"I thought we could all go…"

A whole host of new thoughts started zipping through my mind on overdrive. "Why would we all go?"

"So that it's not one adult and two kids on a camping trip." She sipped again. "Plus, we can work on our co-parenting," she said coyly and it felt like flirting. It was like I was in grade school all over again and Jessica Hardin was approaching my desk with a Valentine clutched in her hands and my heart was beating out of my chest. "Jack said you both have a tent, Abbie and I both have a tent, the holiday weekend is coming up–"

"No." I needed to stop this before it got any further. "I don't even think Jack is going to be around this summer. She's definitely in line for boot camp," I said seriously, but it was an empty, meaningless threat.

The line went quiet for a couple of seconds and then a very pleasant, "I'll murder you on Abbie's behalf if you do that," breathed into the receiver.

I laughed. "You don't even like camping."

"That's not true and you know it."

I knew it wasn't true. She loved camping. "You never went with me," I muttered.

"It wasn't an option then," she said softly. "Kate, the girls really want to go."

I threw up my free hand in the air, pleading with Lauren, the universe, or anyone else who would listen, but it was futile. I was my only witness. "I'm so glad the whims of our children are dictating our lives."

"Will you at least think about it? If I would've asked you to go camping in college, you would have already driven to my house with sleeping bags," she said matter-of-factly.

"A lot has changed over the years," I reminded her. *The cooler would have been packed too.*

"You keep telling yourself that," she said just loud enough for me to hear, but quietly enough so that I'd let it go. I did. "Just think about it." She released a soft hum-sigh.

I closed my eyes and held the phone as she sipped her whiskey neat, because that's how I taught her how to drink it years ago, and the rest of the world fell off its edge.

"Lauren?" I asked the comfortable silence to which I received no response. "Thank you for being there for Jack."

"You don't need to thank me. Jack is one of the most important people in my life because she's your daughter. I'll always be there for her."

"I know that."

"You know…if we tried, it would always be like this."

"Emergency room visits and me threating hospital staff?" I interjected to deflect, but she didn't laugh.

"We make a good team."

"You mean forced group work?"

"*We* make a good team."

I wanted to argue, but I couldn't. "I know we do." *We always have.*

CHAPTER THIRTY-NINE

I rummaged through all of our bags, but no matter how hard I looked, I couldn't find my tent. "Jack, I asked you to pack my tent. You said you packed it…" I heard the distinct sound of two ten-year-olds giggling uncontrollably. When I turned around, Jack and Abbie were side by side and looked as thick as thieves.

"Maybe you and my mom could share a tent," Abbie said through another giggle.

My mouth hung open in utter disbelief. I had been played by third-graders. I narrowed my eyes. "Or maybe Jack and I can share a tent and you and your mother can share a tent." I raised a single eyebrow in a challenge.

"Mom, no." Abbie turned to Lauren in protest.

I turned to Jack. "Baby," the soft-stern word escaped and I knew that I had her full attention. "Did you purposely not pack my tent?"

Jack said nothing and studied the laces on her shoes and I was transported back to when I taught her how to tie them. *Over, under, pull it tight, make a bow, do it right.*

"We can stand here all day," I said after a few tense moments of silence.

"Yes."

"Why?"

"It was my idea, Kate." Abbie rushed out, jumping to Jack's defense.

"Abbie," Lauren reprimanded.

"Abbie, shut up," Jack hissed.

"Language," I said to Jack. The first moment that we had alone, I was going to explain never using those two words when speaking to a woman ever again, especially one that she was interested in. "Why?" I asked again, tilting her chin gently until she met my eyes.

Jack looked quickly at Abbie and then back to me. "Maybe you could date Ms. Dawson and then Abbie and I could hang out all the time."

I could tell that she was desperate to look down at her laces, but she held my gaze. I was proud of her. My daughter had the heart of a lion, although sometimes a bit misplaced. "You can't force two people to be together. It happens or it doesn't. Do you understand? How would you feel if I forced you to sleep in a tent with a boy? You'd hate that."

"But you like Lauren," Jack announced for all the campground to hear like she was citing scripture. Had she held two stone tablets in her hands, I would have been convinced that the lake would have parted. I would have welcomed it at that moment. "I heard you tell Patricia that you have feelings for Lauren."

I closed my eyes briefly and then turned to look at the lake. No matter how hard I tried to part the waters with my mind so that they would crash down upon me, it simply wouldn't happen, I didn't have Jack's command. *Pity.*

"*You like my mom!*" Abbie squealed while she jumped up and down, snapping me out of my daydream nightmare.

I didn't dare look at Lauren. I could only imagine the Cheshire-like grin plastered across her face and I could do without seeing that for a few more seconds. Instead, I looked up to the heavens in search of God or her understudy. Only she could save me now. Jack wouldn't be so lucky. "*Jacquelyn Elizabeth Connors*," I said deliberately. "I suggest you go and play somewhere quietly, while I decide if we're still staying here for the weekend."

She quickly grabbed Abbie's hand and ran out of sight.

I stood rooted to my spot, my face flushed with emotion. It felt like an out-of-body experience. All I could hear was the faint chirping of the birds in the background and the blood rushing through my ears, it was a symphony.

"Kate—" Lauren started to say.

I cut her off, shaking my head as I continued to look for answers to questions that I didn't possess and probably never would. "Don't say anything right now, not a single word, I beg of you." I unrooted myself and in a daze stumbled over to the picnic table until I was sitting on the top with my feet resting on the bench.

Lauren joined me. "You can't be mad at them. It's cute."

"Says the women with the tent." I finally turned to her for the first time in minutes. "If you didn't have somewhere to sleep tonight, I doubt you'd be thrilled about the situation."

She tilted her head to the side, like she was studying a last-place, second grade, science experiment. She rested her hand on my knee, skin on skin, and her fingerprints burned into my flesh. "I'd just sleep in your tent." She said it like it she was reciting the alphabet, simple and succinct.

My eyes widened and I leaned back slightly as I studied her expression. "That's awfully bold of you. What makes you think I'd invite you?" I asked with a smirk, finally getting some of my bearings back.

"You have *feelings* for me," she said in a sing-song voice, squeezed my knee, got up and walked away. Although her back was toward me, I knew without a doubt that the Cheshire-like grin had returned.

"Mom, are you really going to sleep out here?" Jack asked with concern in her voice.

"I hope the bears don't eat me."

"Bears," Abbie said quietly.

"Kate," Lauren reprimanded.

"You're right, the bears aren't anywhere near here." I looked quickly over my shoulder pretending that I had heard a noise. "I've got to watch out for tigers."

"There aren't tigers in the woods," Jack said through a half-unsure laugh. "Are there tigers, Ms. Dawson?"

"Jack, I'm pretty sure I heard about a sighting last week," I said quickly before Lauren could spoil all of my fun. "Bedtime for you guys." I looked over my shoulder again pretending to hear another noise.

"I don't want you to get eaten by a tiger." Jack's eyes started to water.

"I really wish I had my tent. I'm pretty sure it had tiger repellant in it…"

"*Kate.*"

The party was over. "I'm just pulling your leg, kiddo. There are no bears and no tigers. I wouldn't let anything get into our camp, okay? I want you to go to bed and I'll see you in the morning."

"Do you promise?" Jack asked.

I held up two fingers. "Scout's honor."

Lauren nudged my foot. "You were never a scout."

"Scout's honor," I said again and stuck out my tongue.

"Night, Mom. I love you. Night, Ms. Dawson."

"Love you too, baby."

"Good night, Mom." Abbie leaned in for a kiss from Lauren.

As the girls closed up their tent and settled in for the night, I picked up a stick and poked the fire.

"It's ridiculous that you make Jack call me by my last name and Abbie by your first name."

"You have a lot of unsolicited parenting advice. It's only manners. We don't really have a lot of other rules, but that's one of them."

I stood and put a couple of more logs on the fire. I watched as the flames welcomed them; it was almost hypnotic. I got completely lost in the dance and for a moment a calmness settled over my soul. My trepidation for this trip was unfounded. This was going to be fine. It was a beautiful night, the sky was full of stars, and the fire was crackling and close. When I looked at Lauren, her attention was not on the night sky or the roaring fire, but on me with an unreadable expression. I held her gaze and I refused to let it go.

"Are you really sleeping out here tonight?"

"That's the plan."

"You can sleep in my tent." There was no flirtation in her statement. It was a genuine offer because no doubt she had taken pity on me and my predicament.

"Thank you for your offer, but it's okay. I've had worse sleeping conditions."

"Don't trust yourself around me?" And just like that the innuendo was back. I had to at least give her some credit. She'd waited a whole millisecond.

"If I recall correctly, I was always very well behaved around you. I always kept my hands to myself." I pointed to her with an accusing finger. "It was your hands that couldn't be trusted."

"If I didn't make a move, nothing would have ever happened between us. You would have let it all play out in your mind."

I was taken aback for a moment as there was such a sad truth in that statement. "At least we would have had a happy ending," I said quietly.

It was true. Had nothing happened between us, it would have just been a fantasy, a series of *what-if's* that I would have conjured in my mind, but it would have ended on a happy note. No matter how hard I tried after the fact, I couldn't manufacture happily ever after, even in my dreams. Every time I tried, there were too many pitfalls, dragons, and trolls waiting under the bridge to dash my hopes. I wasn't angry or bitter; I had just come to accept the fate of this reality years ago.

"It's going to get cold tonight."

"I promise, I'll be fine. I'll sleep in the car if it gets too cold."

"Suit yourself." She stood, walked to her tent and zipped it up.

I listened as she puttered inside. There was a moment when I thought the zipper would open, but nothing happened, and all noise ceased. I tossed a couple of more logs onto the fire, unfurled my sleeping bag next to the hot stones and laid down with my hands propping up the back of my head.

It had been a long drive and an even longer day. Sleep would come eventually, but for now my mind raced. What steps had I taken in my life to get to this precise moment? Was each moment a predetermined star acting as a roadmap across the night sky? If I removed one of the stars, would I be heading in a completely different direction? Perhaps. Which star was it that led me back to this town, to this moment, to Lauren? Was it work? Had it always been meant to fail? Was it Jack? Was she the key? These felt like questions that I was meant to bounce off someone, but the only someone that I wanted to bounce them off of I didn't fully trust anymore. I couldn't say any of this to Lauren. She'd read too much into it, and if she didn't... I'd be hurt.

As the night wore on, I shivered uncontrollably inside my sleeping bag. I refused to go to the car as I knew I wouldn't fare any better. I would kill Jack when we got home. I warred with myself, weighing all of my options. I could wake up Abbie and move her to Lauren's tent. I could kick both girls out of their tent and make them sleep in the car, or the least appealing option possible, I could suck up the better parts of my pride and sleep in Lauren's tent.

I finally stood and gathered my sleeping bag. I walked over to the girls' tent, counted to three, but I couldn't do it. If I woke them up, they would never get back to sleep. I wanted to scream into my sleeping bag. I walked over to Lauren's tent and as quietly as I could, unzipped it and snuck inside. I could see the silhouette of her sleeping form, but she didn't move. Only after I could hear the soft sound of her breathing, did I unfurl my sleeping bag a few feet from where she slept and crawled inside. I laid on my side, away from her, and waited for my body to warm up as it shivered uncontrollably. A second later, I heard the rustling of Lauren's sleeping bag as it moved toward me. Her arm wrapped around my waist and pulled me close. I immediately stiffened at the contact. She brought her mouth to my ear and whispered, "If you wanted to role-play movie scenarios, you should have told me. Of course, you would pick the sad movie. Dibs on playing Ennis," she playfully teased into my ear, and I was well on my way to heating up.

"Lauren." I started to protest as I tried to wiggle out of her grasp, but she held firm.

"Shut up, Kate." Jack wasn't the only one who I needed to have a conversation with. "I've listened to you shiver for the last two hours. I'm exhausted. The quicker you warm up, the quicker I can get to sleep."

"You're the most selfish woman I know," I said into the small confines of the tent.

As my body relaxed, I didn't overthink it. I couldn't. I never would have gotten to sleep. I pushed the natural fragrance of Lauren from my mind. I pushed the proximity of her mouth to my ear into another universe altogether. The only thing I allowed was the warmth from her body and the beating of her heart, which felt so much quicker than my own.

As I started to drift off, another whisper crossed my cheek. "Do you still have feelings for me?"

It would have been so easy to just say yes, but I couldn't, not tonight. "Lauren... When have I ever talked about my feelings? Jack misheard." It was a lie but there was enough of the truth in it to stop and make her think. I never once told her how I felt. I never had the luxury. I was on borrowed time and I wasn't going to use rushed moments to tell her that I was half the woman I wanted to be without her. I lied because what else was I going to do in a tiny tent that was only ever meant for one person?

"Kate—"

"Shhh." I pushed my body back against her. "Go to sleep." And we did.

* * *

"Does everyone have their hiking buddy?"

Jack and Abbie held up their clasped hands together and Lauren blew me a kiss.

We opted for the trail around the lake with the girls in front of us. Scenic and simple. A perfect way to kick off the trip in earnest.

"You're not my hiking buddy," I said as we went along.

She laughed. "Then you struggle with basic math."

Even though it was the holiday weekend, it didn't feel like the grounds were overcrowded with campers, which suited me just fine. I watched as Jack and Abbie pointed out different things to one another. It was sweet and despite all the turmoil prior to the trip, I was happy that they had the opportunity to make these memories together.

"What are you thinking about?"

I pointed ahead of us and Lauren nodded in agreement.

"What are you thinking about?" I asked after a few minutes, when a comfortable silence settled between us.

"About yesterday."

"What about it?"

"About you telling Patricia that you had feelings for me…"

"I told you, it didn't happen."

"Then why would Jack say it?"

I pinched the bridge of my nose. Jack was in serious trouble when we got home, Abbie or no Abbie. "She misunderstood an adult conversation."

"What was the conversation about?"

I could have just told her to mind her own business and continued the rest of the trail without my hiking buddy, but she was going to hear the news sooner or later. "We broke up."

"When?"

"A while ago."

"Why didn't you say anything?"

I shrugged. "You got sick, Jack fell, we were getting ready for this weekend. It wasn't breaking news or anything. I told you, she and I were just casual."

"So, a proper breakup? At least she got to hear you say goodbye."

"I did say goodbye to you."

"You know what I mean."

I stopped walking, but my eyes stayed on the girls ahead of us. I knew she was talking about when I left town without saying a word. "I didn't think you'd care."

"That is absolute garbage and you know it. You did it to hurt me and it did."

"No, not everything is about you. I did it so that I wouldn't hurt anymore."

"That worked so well, didn't it?" She sighed deeply and I could tell that she regretted her words. "You're not the only one that hurts, Kate."

"What do you want from me?"

"The truth."

I shook my head and sighed. "You think you do, but it gets us nowhere. I did tell Patricia that I have feelings for you. I have always had feelings for you. I will always have feelings for you, but it doesn't mean that I know what to do with them. You lied. You swore up and down that you wanted to be with me. You made promises about the future. And I get it. We were kids. How can I possibly hold you to that now? But I believed in you, in us. It is so difficult for me to reconcile those two versions of you, and now you're this different person."

"I'm not–"

"Yes, you are. You've become this extraordinary woman, and I don't know what to do with any of it."

She stood there stunned.

I shrugged and continued on without my hiking buddy.

Lauren and I sat on top of the picnic table as the girls sat on a sleeping bag facing the lake. We watched the fireworks light up the sky. Unfortunately, the popping of the yellow, red, and green lights was the furthest thing from my mind. Tomorrow we would be leaving and it was a sad realization. It felt like this trip, the four of us together, was somehow exactly where each one of us was supposed to be. I looked down at Jack, who sat cross-legged next to Abbie, their little hands clasped together between their bodies. I immediately froze. I leaned over to Lauren and pointed between the two.

She turned to me with a "well-duh" expression on her face, and I felt like that last place science experiment all over again. "And? They've been doing that for a while now."

I pointed up to the sky and then back to their hands, trying to make my point. "Never during fireworks."

"This is the only time they've watched fireworks together."

"Don't you feel like this is moving too fast. They're ten, Lauren. Am I the only one that has a problem with this?"

"*Yes*," she practically yelled.

The girls looked over at us and then Lauren pulled me away from the picnic table.

"I can assure you, you're the only one that has a problem with this. It's cute. So they like each other. It's completely innocent. Jack would never do anything to make Abbie uncomfortable."

"She would never do that." I gave Lauren a shocked expression.

"I know, I'm telling you that." She gently smacked me upside the head. "And Abbie would never."

"She would never," I said quickly, ready to defend that mastermind's honor.

Lauren smacked me again. "Just relax about it."

"I think I need to say something to Jack."

"About what?"

"That I see the hand holding."

"Don't say *anything* about it. You're going to draw too much attention to it. Leave it alone. They're just kids. It will fade out, or in a few years…it's a different conversation."

Her words sounded incredibly logical, but it felt like inaction wasn't the right move in this situation. At an early age, Jack had said she thought girls were pretty. It was hard for me to argue. She knew that I dated women, but I never brought anyone home, because right or wrong, I didn't want to influence her or who she was going to become. I wanted her to figure that out for herself, with a little help and guidance from me. It felt like we were on the cusp of a moment and I needed to say something.

"Jack, can you come over here for a second?"

She got up from the blanket and stood in front of me. I held out my hands for her and she took them. I gave them a reassuring squeeze.

"It's okay to hold Abbie's hand."

"I know. I like holding Abbie's hand." She smiled and looked over to Abbie as the fireworks danced across the sky.

I felt bad for taking her away from the moment, but I needed to make sure that we were both on the same page. I squeezed her hands again. "But that's it. Holding hands. That's it."

She scrunched her eyebrows together. "I can hug Abbie, right?" she asked unsure.

"Of course, there's nothing wrong with hugging. A hug for hello. A hug for goodbye. Special occasions…" I started to ramble.

Lauren elbowed me in the ribs.

"But nothing other than hugging."

"What else would we do?" She eyed me carefully.

"Absolutely nothing if you ever want to see each other again."

"Way to go, genius." Lauren laughed and walked away.

When the girls were tucked safely away in their tent, Lauren and I sat by a fire that had started to die and I had no desire to stoke. The dying embers meant one thing; I was that much closer to sharing a one-person tent with Lauren again. I had ignored her persistent yawning for the last five minutes.

"Are you coming soon?" she asked.

"In a bit."

"I'm not going to bite…although I do recall you enjoying that."

"Lauren—"

"We're on vacation. It's our last night, loosen up."

I turned to her with a sweet smile. "I'll be in shortly, dear, as soon as I finish up these dishes and take the dog for a walk."

"We're role-playing an old married couple tonight?" She laughed and it was hard not to follow her lead. "Your kinks have certainly changed over the years."

"Go to bed. I'll be in soon. I'm just going to put out the fire."

I took my time. I wanted to wait until she drifted off. I could sleep beside her. It was difficult but manageable if she was sleeping. I crawled in beside her sleeping form, which was turned away from me, and I settled into my sleeping bag. My heart pounded and I started to count every beat like it was a little sheep jumping over a white picket fence.

"What are you thinking about?" Lauren's whispered words interrupted my sequence and one of my poor little heartbeats slammed headfirst into the last board of the fence.

"I thought you were sleeping?"

"I pretended to sleep so you would get in here and magically it worked."

"Are you calling me predictable?"

"Nothing about you is predictable."

I said nothing and started to count my beats again.

"Last night here... The fireworks were nice."

"The whole weekend was nice. You know, I feel like I'm chaperoning my daughter's big epic childhood romance. If both of them don't end up somewhere on the spectrum it's going to just devastate the other."

"I know. Are you going to want to get back early tomorrow?"

"I think it makes the most sense, so we'll beat traffic."

"Are you going to swim before we go?" she asked.

"If I get up early enough."

"I liked your bathing suit..."

"*Lauren.*"

"What?" She rolled over to face me. "I can't say that?"

"You can, but you probably shouldn't."

"I wish I still looked that good..."

I put my finger over her lips and then cursed myself for the decision. I hadn't felt anything softer in the last fifteen years. "You're gorgeous. You've always been gorgeous. These..." I reached up and brushed my fingertips near the side of her face, where a couple of fine lines were near the corner of her eye.

"My wrinkles."

"No, your laugh lines." I removed my fingers when I realized that I was still touching her and tucked my hand inside my sleeping bag.

"What about them?" she asked after a moment.

"They are the best things since sliced bread."

"White or whole wheat?"

"The best," I whispered. It took every ounce of self-restraint not to lean over and place a kiss where my fingertips had just touched seconds before.

"Why?"

"Because you have the most amazing laugh and it means that you did. It means that you were happy and it warms my heart."

"Kate?"

"Yes?"

"I wasn't happy without you."

I blew out an unsteady breath but said nothing and we let the moment pass.

I never got to sleep that night.

CHAPTER FORTY

After we returned from our camping trip, the girls were busy finishing up school and Lauren and I were in the process of gearing down for what would hopefully be a quiet summer. I had dropped off Jack at Abbie's hours ago and decided to catch up on some errands while Lauren had the girls. I hadn't had a free night to myself in a while.

I was making my way through the produce aisle, when I heard Jack's excited voice call out, "Mom!" Lauren pushed a cart in my direction with Jack hanging off one side and Abbie hanging off the other. *My three girls.* Before I could shake the thought away, it was replaced by a different one, as I realized there was something wrong with this picture; there were one too many grocery carts—mine.

"Are you guys stalking me? What are you doing here?"

"They wanted to make brownies, so we're picking up some supplies." Lauren pointed to the contents of her buggy.

"Brownies?" I peered in at the ingredients. "Now I wish I was sleeping over too."

"Oh, Kate, you should," Abbie said happily. "But we don't have a third bed." She looked over at Lauren.

"We'd find *somewhere* to put her," Lauren said dryly and it took everything in me not to burst out laughing.

"Thanks for the offer, but I don't want to cramp Jack's style." I winked at Jack. "Have fun tonight."

"Call me if you change your mind," Lauren said over her shoulder.

As they walked away, my gaze remained fixed, until I was rudely interrupted from my thoughts by the clearing of a throat. When I turned, Betty was a few feet behind me with a grocery basket tucked under her arm. "Shame what happened to her and her husband."

"Betty, don't gossip," I chided softly.

"It's not gossip. Did you know that he—"

I cut her off immediately. "Betty," I said as sternly as I could without being rude. "I don't want to know. She's my friend. I don't want to talk about Lauren behind her back."

She turned from Lauren and focused her attention on a display of grapes. She picked one out of the bunch, put it in her mouth, chewed thoughtfully and then put a different bunch into her basket.

"I've lived here my whole life. I remember when you went to school here. You worked in the stacks at the library."

"You came in every Saturday morning to read all of the different papers."

"I get them on my iPad now," she smiled, like she was letting me in on some technological secret. "You were always so helpful." Her smile softened. "You absolutely devastated that poor girl when you left." She gave me a pointed look and this time she was letting in me on a completely different secret.

My smile slipped and I looked over to Lauren. "That poor girl was married. What do you want me to say?"

"Nothing, dear." She placed her hand on my forearm and gave it a squeeze. "You don't have to say anything. Just..."

"What?"

"It was obvious then, Kate." She squeezed again. "It's obvious now." She put one more grape in her mouth and walked over to the checkout as my mouth hung slightly open.

My phone rang as I sat in bed with a book in my lap. I rummaged through the sheets and blankets and when I flipped it over, Lauren's number flashed across the screen.

"You didn't call," she said quietly when I answered the phone.

"Nope, the couch didn't seem appealing." I tossed my book off to the side. It was a lost cause as I was only half paying attention. My mind was preoccupied on Betty's parting words. How did she know?

"You wouldn't have slept on the couch."

"Now you tell me…" I said dramatically into the phone like it was the only reason keeping me away and not all these years of repressed feelings and resentment.

"I saved you one."

"A brownie?" I asked excitedly.

"A spot in my bed." She lingered on the last word. It felt like she was flirting, which was impossible, considering it was only one syllable. She absolutely mystified me.

"I didn't know it required saving," I flirted back. "You know I like women who play hard to get," I teased, allowing myself the small indulgence. "Why are you up?"

"I was thinking…" I waited patiently. I could hear her even breathing, the sheets rustling. "What's your favorite memory of us?"

"Lauren…" My voice was so half-hearted that she completely ignored me and I couldn't blame her.

"Humor me."

I settled back against my pillows. "You'll think it's silly," I responded through a sigh.

"Tell me."

I flipped through all of my favorite memories to make sure that I had settled on the right one. "The night you invited me to Drew's party. When I had my arms wrapped around you and you asked me about the benefits of the book club. At that moment, a feeling washed over me, and I've never felt it since." The admission felt almost too honest.

There was a silence over the line like she was replaying the memory, savoring it for a moment, and then, "Tell me another one."

I wanted to tell her all of them. I wanted to recite my top ten Lauren and Kate moments, but I hadn't done that in ages, and every time I'd done it in the past, I felt like I needed therapy afterward, or a good hug. I didn't want to do it with her. "I would, but…"

"But what?"

"I don't trust those memories anymore. I've replayed and recycled them a million times over, and surely I've mixed up the facts and changed the outcome. I read an article about that once, about why we shouldn't trust our memories, especially the ones that we tend to overthink…"

"What if we both remember?"

There was something in her voice that sounded like an ache. I desperately wanted to soothe it with sound and touch, but I knew that in doing so I would expose my healed wounds to a potential firing squad. "Wouldn't it be easier if we both forgot?" I asked, but I didn't want an answer to that question.

I was grateful when she let it evaporate. "I saved you a brownie."

"That's my girl," I let slip and neither one of us seemed to mind. "You always knew the way to my heart." A second slip as I smiled into the phone.

"I'll send it home with Jack." She paused and then hesitated. "Do you want to know what my favorite memory of us is?"

"No," I said quietly as I closed my eyes and clutched the phone tightly in my hand.

"Why not?" There was no mistaking the disappointment in her voice as it filled up my room.

"Because… What if it's one that I've finally managed to forget?"

At that moment, my bedroom felt like the quietest place on earth. I could distinctly hear the blood pumping through my veins. As the noise started to overwhelm me, the next sound sliced the air wide open: the line went dead. I studied the display on my phone and then tossed it into the sheets, where I hoped that it would stay buried forever. I settled into the mattress but sleep never came.

CHAPTER FORTY-ONE

The dice clattered together between my palms as three sets of eyes carefully watched the motion, waiting impatiently for me to roll. I blew on my hands for emphasis, which earned me a smile, a giggle, and an eye roll. I released the dice and they danced across the board, knocking over Abbie's thimble.

"Seven," I triumphantly declared and moved the Scottie dog down the board, dodging Jack's hotels and Lauren's houses, landing squarely on Chance. "Phew," I blew out a breath and pretended to wipe my brow. I reached for the neat stack of cards and brought one close to my chest so that no one could see. I read the card to myself and then held it out proudly. "Get out of jail free," I announced and they all collectively groaned.

"You never land on anyone's property," Lauren huffed as she rolled the dice across the board.

"Mom, why did I have to be the bank?" Jack asked.

"Because I'm notorious for stealing from the bank. I'm a rogue banker, but I've raised you better. I know you won't steal."

"You never cheated when we played before," Lauren said for my ears only.

"We played a *much* different version of this game, where the ups and downs in the housing market really didn't come into play," I said quietly to her and then looked over at the girls. "You both need to start getting ready for bed. It's way past your bedtime."

"We're not even halfway through the game." Jack pointed to the board, as she held a stack of money in one hand and half of the properties in the other. She wasn't a bad banker. If anything she was Robin Hood, slipping twenties to Abbie when she thought no one was looking.

"No one ever finishes this game. It's not meant to have a winner. Bedtime." I gestured over to Abbie with my head and then back to Jack. "Abbie's getting tired. Teeth and bed."

Another eye roll from my daughter, but soon after, both of them were on their way up to bed.

Lauren watched me from her spot on the couch, her arms wrapped around a pillow, as I organized the board. "I should get going."

"No one is asking you to leave," she said as she continued to sink further into the cushions. I kept my attention focused on putting the game back in the box, because if I didn't, and my gaze drifted back over in her direction, it would have been far too tempting not to curl up with her and drift off.

"You're tired and it's late. I need to get going."

"Do you want me to make you a coffee?"

"I'm okay." I shrugged back into my sweater that I had discarded hours earlier. "Thanks for inviting me. This was fun."

"Board games are always more fun with four people."

"We had fun in college," I said absentmindedly as the memory flashed. I could distinctly recall half the pieces missing, no dollar bills and only two Community Chest cards, but still, we made it work. Not a difficult task when the game essentially descended into strip Monopoly with hundreds of dollars sitting in Free Parking. That afternoon we broke all the rules and I felt like a little bit like a rebel, while Lauren grinned as article after article of clothing came off.

Her eyes sparkled in the recall. Her mouth was hidden behind a large fluffy pillow, but I could tell that she was smiling.

"We're having pancakes tomorrow morning if you want to come back," the pillow mumbled.

"I don't like pancakes."

"I know, but just come for coffee or… You could take the couch and be here first thing. I promise it's more comfortable than what you had in college." She patted the empty spot beside her and I was transfixed.

"You never once slept on my couch."

"I'd ask you to stay in my bed…"

"You know I can't."

"Actually, I have no idea why you can't. I keep thinking about sleeping beside you in the tent, how long it had been."

"You promised me after that weekend that you wouldn't bring it up."

She shrugged and squeezed the pillow. "If not my bed, then the couch, just stay. It's just a couch, Kate." Her hand moved over the soft white linen. I ignored the action as best as I could and focused on her eyes.

"If it was just a couch, you wouldn't be looking at me like that."

"How am I looking at you?"

"Like you're Wile E. Coyote and you've just laid out a huge pile of birdseed. I'm the Road Runner and I'm debating whether or not I want to eat it, and you're sitting there thinking, 'Today may finally be my day.'"

"You want to eat it?" She wiggled her eyebrows.

"You'll never catch me." I stuck out my tongue.

She threw the pillow in my direction and I dodged it easily.

"Wile E. Coyote always caught the Road Runner."

"Never happened." I crossed my arms.

"It's true. Think about it. The Road Runner always kept coming back for more. Why would he do that? He was already caught."

"Are you going to drop an anvil on my head?"

"Let's hope for your sake that it never comes to that." She smiled. "You wanted to leave…" She looked back at the large clock on the wall. "…Ten minutes ago, but here you are." She folded her hands behind her head and looked up at me with a smirk. I wanted to kiss it away and I knew that it was time for me to leave.

"Good night, Lauren," I said as I started to walk past the sofa.

I never expected her hand to reach out and grab my wrist. "*Stay*."

"I can't—"

"Shhh..." She brought her finger up to her lips. "There's a voice inside your head that wants this. You should listen to her." She squeezed my wrist and let go. "Besides, we deserve an ending."

I knit my eyebrows together. "We have an ending. I'll give you the Coles Notes version. Kate moved away—"

"Ran away."

"I don't need an editor."

"You clearly do. Your history is revisionist and lacking."

"Kate—" I began again.

"*Ran away*," she said slowly and deliberately and I let it be.

It was a point of contention that we could have spent the next ten years debating and continued with my story. "To the city and became—"

"Miserable."

I offered an eye roll, but it was only half-hearted. "A lawyer."

"You should never lead with the fact that you're a lawyer." She stuck out her tongue.

"Lauren stayed behind—"

"And struggled to fix a failed marriage."

"They both had daughters."

"A little ditty..." She hummed the first chords to "Jack and Diane" and winked.

"One day the cat came back," I continued referring to myself.

"She just couldn't stay away."

"Who has a revisionist history now? Their daughters became—"

"Best friends and drew them back together."

I stuck an imaginary pencil in the air as I pretended to contemplate Lauren's last sentence. "Author's correction." I used my finger to strike through Lauren's words and corrected the story, "Enabled them to finally have a friendship. The End."

"That's not how it ends. Where's the romance?"

"Romance? What's an appropriate ending? Happily ever after? You didn't want that. They rode off into the sunset? I tried that. We aren't one of your romance novels," I scoffed.

"Maybe not, but we've got potential. We deserve an ending…a happy one. And we finally have a chance."

I stood before her. A million words waited on the tip of my tongue, but the longer I stood rooted, the ones that I wanted to use wouldn't move past my lips. "I can't. We've found a balance. We've found a way to exist together in this life. This is exactly who we're supposed to be. No more and no less."

CHAPTER FORTY-TWO

"Do you want to do something this weekend?" Lauren asked as I swirled the chocolate-vanilla latte round and round at the bottom of my cup.

I flipped through my mental calendar. "This weekend? The girls have a sleepover at Aaron's. It's already pretty busy, don't you think?" I paused. "I mean, we've got Sunday free. You know Abbie's been showing a real interest in art lately. Maybe the gallery in the city on Sunday morning? We could go after we pick them up, have a light lunch and be back before it's too late. What about that?"

Through my ramble, she carefully rested her chin in her palm. She watched me, half amused and half something else. "I love it when you co-parent." Her infectious smile dazzled me. "But that's not what I meant. Do you want to do something this weekend, specifically Saturday night, when we both have a free night, together?"

"Just the two of us?" I asked strangely.

"Some people may call it a date, but not me because I know how much it would freak you out."

"I don't know why we would do that. What happened to no more and no less?"

"Only you agreed to that ridiculous proposition. If we did go out, we could finally find a reason to justify the fact that you come to my coffee shop every day, or that I pop into the library if you don't. Or that we spend most weekends together anyway with the girls."

"*Pfft*," I made an exasperated sound. "That's not true."

"I'm the only person that you spend time with."

"Fake news." I winked.

"Who else do you spend time with?"

"Jack," I said quickly and she raised her eyebrows. "Abbie." Earned me a snort. "I spend time with Betty."

She laughed and shook her head. "It's a good thing that I didn't ask you out on a date. I may start to get a complex."

"Don't get a complex. You're far too lovely for that."

She looked away and the words blurted out. "Why don't you want me anymore?"

It felt like all the air had been sucked out of the shop. I didn't want to answer her question because it was the furthest thing from the truth, but still, there was a truth in it. "I'm enjoying our friendship. I don't want to fuck it up again. Dating," I scoffed loudly. "News flash for you. We never dated before and I can end the suspense right now. I'm not a good date."

I watched as a quick flash of anger crossed her features, but just as quickly as it came, it was gone.

"I get nervous and quiet on first dates; you'd end up doing most of the talking. Then I'd feel bad and ask you ridiculous questions about coffee beans or something completely trivial, which would make it seem like I'm disinterested, but I would be anything but…" I realized that I had said far too much.

"Where do I sign up?" she asked, as she played with the rim of her coffee cup.

I shook my head.

She reached over, put her hand over mine and held it. "I'll end the suspense right now; I'm not going to hurt you again."

I shrugged. "You don't know that. All we can do is *hope*, but even that is just a series of fleeting beliefs..." I bit down on my lip. "You lied to me..."

"I never lied to you."

"Yes, you did. You told me you wanted to be with me. You told me you were leaving him."

She shook her head and blew out a breath. "You're missing some critical facts, and that's my fault. Let me explain."

"I don't want to hear it. It doesn't change anything."

"You don't even know what it is."

"It changes nothing."

She removed her hand and I instantly missed the warmth that had started to soak in.

We hadn't even gotten to three Mississippis yet.

"Okay, I'll stop pushing."

"Okay?" I asked confused.

"Someone has been trying to set me up and I've been putting it off, but I think I'm going to call and give it a chance."

The last word echoed in the back of my mind. If Lauren was a duck, that never would have happened. It only would have been said once and then I could have heard it and moved on. Instead it bounced off every damn surface in the café. "Good." I put out my fist to fist-bump her.

She tilted her head, her hand remaining planted on the top of the table.

I let my fist explode into nothingness and dropped it into my lap. My shoulders slumped as a wave of panic washed over me, but I tempered my emotions as best as I could. "That's a good idea," I said firmly. "If you make it the night of the girl's sleepover, I can take them over together. It will give you some more time to get ready." It was the last thing that I wanted to say, so of course, I said it.

She tipped her cup back and drained the last drops and looked at me. "Only one of us is going to have regrets when this is all said and done, and it's not going to be me; I tried."

"Lauren—" I reached for her hand, but it was too late, she was already up and out of her seat.

"It's going to be worse than before."

It was a veiled threat, but I knew what she was talking about. I had lived it. *Not fucking possible*.

"It is."

I shook my head back and forth. "Okay, I'll bite, Lauren. Why is it going to be worse?"

"Because one day you'll wake up and realize that *you* pushed me away this time. When you come to that realization, it's going to be so much worse for you than it was before."

"You have no idea what it was like for me," I said quickly, with fifteen years of bitterness edging out.

"It doesn't matter now, does it? None of it matters. I need to get back to work." She walked behind the counter and out of sight.

CHAPTER FORTY-THREE

I picked up the phone for what felt like the thousandth time, debating my options, but then I remembered that I did make Lauren an offer. I finally sent her a quick text message.

Are you awake? Can I call you?

Of course, you can call.

"You're up late," she said when she answered the phone.

"I guess." I picked at a loose thread on the blanket covering my knees.

"So?" she asked after a few quiet moments. "You wanted to talk," she reminded me.

"Right. I wanted to call and see if you wanted me to pick Abbie up tomorrow afternoon for Aaron's party? You said that you might have a date…" I waited for her to confirm, but she said nothing. "I said that I could pick up Abbie to give you some more time, remember?"

"No, *you* said that it would be *convenient* if I had a date the night of Aaron's party, the very same night that I asked you out on a date. I tuned you out when you did that."

"*Oh*...thanks," I said annoyed. "You're the one who said that someone had been trying to set you up and that you were going to give it a chance."

"I don't need your help to do it," she said and it was biting.

"I was just trying to be a good friend." That word. I hated that fucking word, so why was I the one saying it so often now?

"I did give it a chance."

"Huh?"

"I went out a couple of nights ago."

"Oh," the word dragged out and got caught on my teeth. I struggled for what I wanted to say next, and then I remembered my upbringing. If you have nothing nice to say, lie. "That's great." I nearly choked.

"It was *nice*," she said softly.

I immediately cringed at her use of that word. "I really don't need any details."

"Why not? Aren't we *friends*?" she challenged.

"The best. Let's get matching necklaces," I said sarcastically and realized how insanely ridiculous I was being—and how obvious. "What was he like?"

I asked as politely as I could, given the circumstances, given that my jaw was almost permanently locked.

"*She* was nice."

"Lauren..." It wasn't biting, but it was a warning. I could hear the details of many things, but not the news of Lauren dating another woman.

"I hired a sitter for Abbie. I would have asked you, but I thought that would have been incredibly insensitive, even cruel. She lives in the city, so it was a bit of a drive to meet her for drinks."

"Lauren," I warned again but my words were immediately cut off and pushed aside.

"When I arrived, she was already waiting, dressed to impress."

There are moments in time, where emotions become magnified, larger than life. This was one of those moments. I could taste my anger. It wasn't directed toward her, but the true wrongdoer, me. "I'm begging you to stop."

"I don't have a gun to your head, Kate. Hang up the phone if you don't want to hear it." She paused and waited for me to do just that, but I couldn't. I needed those facts. I needed to drive past the wreckage on the highway, stop and look, even if it was me behind the damaged wheel.

When she realized that I wasn't going to disconnect, she said, "It was the *very first date* that I had ever been on with another woman, since you recently told me that what you and I did was never considered dating. The sleepovers, the dances, the whiskey, the picnic on your living room floor, when we locked ourselves in the shop. Meaningless non-dates." The bite in her voice was gone and it was replaced with something that I hadn't heard in years—pain.

I held my finger over the end call button, but I couldn't disconnect as hard as I tried.

"Her name is Joanna. She's a little bit older, but not by much. She's a consultant."

I stewed in my own self-induced pot of rage and regret. I would have paired perfectly with a Malbec at that moment. I hated Joanna and everything that she stood for. I thought of all the ways that I could reinstate my legal license, apply to the Crown's office and have *Joanna* incarcerated on some trumped-up white-collar criminal charges.

"We had drinks. The conversation flowed easily. It was simple; it was *nice*. Toward the end of the night, she asked me if I wanted to come and visit her, have dinner at her place, spend the night. She leaned in to kiss me—"

"*Stop*," I practically choked out. "You're being cruel. I'm waving my white flag. I don't want to hear this. I can't hear this."

"This is what *friends* do."

"We're not friends!" Then I remembered where I was, who I was speaking with and the hour.

"Then you lied to me when you said we were. Do you want to know what my favorite memory of us is?"

"No."

"Then hang up the phone."

But I couldn't. It felt like if I didn't, I'd lose her forever.

"Remember when we went out for dinner on one of our *non-dates*?" she asked and there was that pain again. "That little French bistro on First Street?"

I racked my brain, but I couldn't remember us ever going out for dinner.

"It was dimly lit. The waitress seated us near the back of the restaurant and from what I remember it was just the two of us."

The filing cabinet of my brain was empty. *This never happened.*

"It was toward the end… It was the first time we ever went out in public together and your smile was *inoubliable*," she said slowly in French.

My voice caught over the phone. A traitor in my own body, one I would never trust again; I clamped it firmly shut.

"We sat across from one other. After the waitress took our order, you reached across the table for my hands so that you could hold them in yours, and the look on your face was never-to-be-forgotten."

My stomach bottomed out the second it all came flooding back. The music, the lights, the way she looked as she sat across from me. It was the only thing I had managed to forget after all of this time because it hurt too damn much to remember. I felt like I was going to be sick. I opened my mouth to get more air into my lungs, to ward off nausea, but the words had been waiting there. "You pulled your hands away before I could reach them," I said just above a whisper, eyes closed tightly. I was desperate to vanquish the memory once again, but it remained and circled like a merry-go-round. I swallowed painfully against my throat and everything burned within me. I felt like I was going to cry, it would have only been the second time in fifteen years. "Your favorite memory of *us* is one that I buried so deep inside of me to escape it." I gulped down the air. "Your favorite memory of *us*, is me being so happy and then you pulling the rug right from under me?"

"No," she said softly. "It's my favorite memory of us because I knew at that moment that you loved me. That what was happening between us wasn't just an affair. Wasn't just something casual to you. It was bigger than that. You never told me that you loved me, not once, but at that moment I knew because you reached for me. I wish I could have reached out for you. I'd do anything to change that moment, Kate. We have a second chance now."

I shook my head frantically but said nothing.

"I didn't let her kiss me. I couldn't. I told her that it wasn't going to work...that I was still in love with someone, you."

All the wind left my sails and they collapsed helplessly in the stillness. I was destined to float aimlessly in Lauren's never-ending waters for the rest of my life. I couldn't move on with anyone else and there was no safe harbor to rest my boat. I'd die like this. *I'm going to die like this.*

"Say something," Lauren said after it became too awkward not to.

"I'm sorry that I called." I hung up the phone.

CHAPTER FORTY-FOUR

The night of Aaron's party, a calmness settled over me and I was content to sink into the cushions of the couch. My body felt weightless; only my feet firmly planted to the floor, grounded me to the moment. My fingers loosely held onto a tumbler of whiskey perched on top of my knee as it bounced softly up and down. For a second, I smelled the faint scent of lavender as it drifted through the windows. If not for the opening and closing of my front door, I would have drifted off peacefully.

"Your door was open," she said as she walked into the living room.

"Actually...it was closed but unlocked. You had to turn the handle to check and when you found that it was unlocked, you opened it and walked right in."

"Don't you just love small towns?"

"Yes, the never-ending allure of breaking and entering by gorgeous women."

"Do you want this gorgeous woman to leave?"

"I never said that." I smiled at her boldness. I absolutely loved that about her.

"Waiting for someone?"

"Nope."

"Is this what you're doing tonight?"

"Yep." I held up my glass in the air.

"This is what you decided to do instead of going out on a date with me?"

I shrugged.

"Want company? I promise I'll do my best to make it not feel like a date."

"What happens if it starts to feel like a date?" I smiled gently to ease some of the tension that had settled into the room and was starting to disrupt the calmness that I had captured only moments ago.

She sat down beside me and reached for my glass and took a sip.

"Do you want your own glass?"

"When did I ever need my own glass with you?"

I had never thought about it, but with the exception of coffee, any other beverage that Lauren ever consumed around me was done out of my glass. When I first met her, she never cared for whiskey, but she'd always reach for my tumbler, making sure that our fingers brushed.

"Think the girls are having fun?"

"Jack's with Abbie. They could be doing math homework and she'd be over the moon." I put my feet up on the coffee table and leaned back against the cushions. "I go back and forth as to whether or not I should be worried about it."

"They're just kids."

"Jack told me that she's going to marry Abbie when she gets older."

"Not if I marry you first." She turned to me and winked.

I cracked a smile and any reasonable objection that I could use to damper her joke was lost in that crack.

"They're really cute."

"Yeah," I sighed. "Until Jack gets her little heart broken."

"Abbie's just as infatuated. It'll lessen over time when they both make some more friends. They'll date girls if they want or boys if they want."

"It takes Jack a while to get over things," I lamented.

"Like her mother?" she asked, but I knew she wasn't taking a shot.

"Yeah, like me. I did get over you."

"Did you?" She put her feet on the corner of my coffee table.

"You are very presumptuous this evening. Walking into my house, helping yourself to my whiskey, feet up on the table, telling me about my feelings. You're the most infuriating woman I know."

"Maybe that's why I still drive you crazy."

"Sometimes I think it was a mistake to come back here, but then I see how happy Jack is with a normal routine and I should have done it years ago." I reached for the glass and took a sip.

"Why a mistake?"

"Too much of the past." I tipped the tumbler in her direction and drained the contents.

"I thought you said you got over me." She took the glass from my hand, reached for the decanter on the coffee table and filled it.

"So bold." I took back my glass and gave her a salute before I had a generous sip. The alcohol's warmth soothed my nerves which were starting to come undone.

"I was upset when you left town. You never said you were leaving."

"It seemed pointless."

A silence settled between us and I closed my eyes momentarily, until her next words. "I thought about you for years. It never stopped."

"We don't need to talk about this."

"I dreamt about being with you."

"I think our date is officially over," I warned.

"I never got over you," she whispered.

I drained the last remnants of the glass. "I did."

"You're lying…"

"No, you lied, Lauren. That's the problem."

She shook her head. "Focus on the present. We have a chance now…"

"No, we don't. I'm not some stupid kid who'd follow you around thinking that you're capable of being with me."

"You used to kiss me like I was going to disappear."

"Stop." I gripped the glass in my hands.

"Your skin was always so warm when I was underneath you."

"Get out of my house," I said quietly, quickly losing control over my emotions.

"When you were inside me…"

"Get the fuck out of my house."

"Make me."

"Make you?" I shook my head. "We're still acting like kids."

I got up from the couch and walked toward the stairs. "Let yourself out." I walked up to my bedroom and slammed the door shut.

A few moments later, the front door slammed shut. I sat down on my bed, head in my hands, as I tried to regulate my breathing. Why couldn't she just leave the past alone? I wanted to pull my hair out in frustration, but I was dragged from my thoughts when the doorknob turned and my bedroom door opened. Lauren looking just as frustrated as I felt, stepped inside the room, closed the door behind her and leaned against it.

We watched one another and became stuck in a staring contest, neither one of us doing or saying anything, until she brought her hands up to her shirt and started to undo the buttons.

"What the *hell* are you doing?"

"Dropping an anvil on your head." She got to the last buttons, pushed the material open, exposing an indigo colored bra. She undid the top button of her jeans and pulled down the zipper. "Tell me that you don't want me."

I blinked rapidly as I took her in, my mouth becoming increasingly parched. I dug my fingernails into the tops of my thighs to break the spell, but the pinch to my skin confirmed that this was no dream. She stepped out of her jeans and tossed them along with her shirt to the floor. She reached behind to unclasp her bra and I raised my hands up in the air. "Don't," I said weakly. It was pitiful, I wouldn't have even listened to me. My resolve was a puddle quickly drying in the hot summer sun when it needed to be an ocean.

She tilted her head and smirked. I knew that it was game over when she undid the clasp and pulled the straps down her shoulders and dropped it to the side. I closed my eyes but that image would stay with me for the rest of eternity. *Fuck me.*

"Do you remember when you made me orgasm from just biting and sucking my nipples that one afternoon?" she asked.

The blood that had started to pool to the lower regions of my body immediately skyrocketed to my ears and I felt flush all over. I shook my head, but of course I remembered *that* afternoon.

"That's only happened to me once in my entire life, *with you.*"

"Why are you doing this?"

"Because if I leave it up to you, *nothing* is ever going to happen. Tell me that you don't want me and I'll stop."

"I don't—"

"Tell me with your eyes open."

When I opened my eyes, her fingers were just creeping past the band in her underwear. I immediately slammed my eyes shut and started to laugh maniacally, my sanity on the verge of completely slipping away forever.

"I have missed you so much." A soft throaty moan escaped her lips.

"Lauren, *I'm begging you…*"

"Open your eyes and deal with it."

I obeyed her command and came face to face with fifteen years of repressed feelings and resentment. "What do you want from me?" I practically cried.

"Everything," she moaned again.

My emotions churned and if I hadn't been sitting on the bed, I would have fallen over. "I offered that once and you didn't want it. It broke me…" I choked on the words. "It's still breaking me." I finally admitted, "I can't lose you again…not this version of you. I'd rather die."

"You aren't going to lose me. Tell me a better way to get your attention and I'll try that. Talking with you isn't working. Reasoning with you isn't working. I'm out of options. Give me a better one."

"This isn't a fair fight."

"You could always get naked too," she suggested playfully.

I looked up to the ceiling and shook my head. "Now I know why you never did anything with your degree. There's a fundamental gap in logic."

"You're staring, Kate."

I screwed my eyes shut.

"I miss you," she choked out. The playfulness in her voice was gone and replaced by something that I didn't recognize. "Touch me…*please*."

The floorboards creaked softly as she moved toward the bed. When she was within an inch of me, I could feel the heat radiating off her body, and it felt as close as something can feel to home without the brick and mortar. If I just kept my eyes closed, perhaps I could wish her away, but then I'd be right back here in another fifteen years lamenting, *if only*. If only I opened my eyes, reached for her, took her in my arms, told her how I felt. Maybe it would be different this time, but then again, maybe not. I was so tired. It felt like I had spent the better part of a decade trying to escape her, but it was impossible because there was one fundamental truth that I couldn't ignore: I didn't want too.

I took my white-knuckled hands and released the tension. I stood and opened my eyes to the light of the early evening and Lauren. The way the shadows danced across her skin made my breath catch. My first touch against her skin was a tremble. How many dreams had I had over the years that had started with her right in front of me, only to have her vanish the very second that I reached out? But she didn't disappear, instead, a soft moan escaped her lips and she pushed closer to the contact. One touch led to two and I was instantly transported back to college and my mapmaking days, where I knew where every freckle resided. Yet as my eyes followed my fingertips, it was clear that things had changed with time. It would take hours to map out the new landmarks and commit them to memory. With every fingerprint against her skin, a revealing shuddered breath left my lungs that my teeth couldn't hold on too, no matter how hard I tried. I was a desperate mess. My movements lacked confidence, like I was an amateur who hadn't been with her or any other woman. I imagine it must have been similar to how she felt our first time.

When she finally touched me, I flinched at the contact, because any other time it had happened over the past fifteen years I had woken up in a cold sweat. The reality of her and this moment was too much for my mind and body. I needed to get some control over the situation or I would lose myself completely.

"This doesn't mean anything," I choked out. I knew it was a lie, but telling her that I had dreamt about this moment thousands of times over only felt like I was opening up myself once again to a heartache that would never ease.

Her fingertips prevented any further words from escaping. "This means *everything*," her voice quivered. Her hands were on my jaw pulling me toward her. When she leaned in to kiss me, I met her halfway. Our lips were light and unsure. When neither one of us made a move to bolt for the doorway, it must have given her the reassurance she needed, because her next kiss was bruising and the summation of fifteen years of lost kisses. My stomach tied in knots, coiling in anticipation with every caress. Her fingers dug into my hipbones until it felt like she was trying to push her prints into the skin so that the marks would sink into the surface and remain forever.

I broke the kiss to catch my breath and my nerves. Her forehead rested against mine. When I felt a teardrop hit my cheek, I opened my eyes and without thinking, leaned forward and kissed it away. She gently shook her head and another escaped. I didn't know what she was feeling at that moment, as I could barely make sense of my own emotions.

"I never thought I'd see you again… I never thought we would be in this moment again…and here we are." She wiped away another tear, and my heart caught in my throat. I pulled her close, wrapped my arms around her and started to sway back and forth to a melody that didn't exist except in my mind. She moved with me, her arms circling around my neck. After a few silent moments, I started to hum the first few notes to "I'll Be Seeing You." She sighed in approval.

We removed my clothing together through the dance until we were in each other's arms, head to toe, skin on skin, without a slip of light passing between us. It felt so different after all this time. We laid on the bed, her on top of me. Her nipples brushed against my own. Her thighs pressed into mine. I brought my mouth to her neck, into her hair, and breathed in as deeply as I could to commit her scent to memory once again. When I inhaled, it filled me up completely, making me light-headed. Lavender and something else hit my senses and after all these years it was suffocating in the most delicious way possible. I pulled her closer still like I was hanging on for dear life. This was enough. This would get me through the next fifteen years. I wanted to move, I wanted to react, I wanted to do something other than anchor myself to her, but I felt frozen in her arms.

She moved her head from my shoulder and brought her lips to my ear. "You're overthinking this," the soft words roared.

I was terrified, not of her, but of everything that this would mean. I couldn't stop the thoughts or the doubts from coming to the forefront. "I don't know what to do." I bit down on my lip to try and stabilize the instability of a heartbeat threatening to spill over. If I moved a muscle and she evaporated, I'd never forgive myself. If I said the wrong thing and she released herself from my arms and left this moment, I'd never utter another word.

She smiled into my skin and gently placed a kiss against the surface. "That was never a problem in college. You always knew what to do. You always knew what to say, even the things you never did. I don't want you to do anything, just feel. My skin on yours, my heart beating against yours. Stop thinking and just feel me in your arms."

Even though I was lying down, it felt like I was trembling on unsteady legs. My joints and bones, the threads that held me together were academic at best. I felt like they would completely unravel with a well-placed whisper from her lips against my skin.

"Just let go."

The words touched my ears and it took a moment for the meaning to register. I loosened my grip fractionally. If I was going to drown, no better time than with her beside me. She nuzzled into my ear and repeated the words over and over. She punctuated each letter into my skin as her lips moved down my body, and when the whisper finally came after fifteen years, I dropped off the edge.

CHAPTER FORTY-FIVE

When I woke up the next morning, Lauren was draped across me. It was everything that I had thought and dreamed about for the past fifteen years. I took a few moments to watch how the morning light danced across her skin, committed it to memory, and then sighed deeply and started to untangle myself from her and the sheets. I slowly eased out of the bed and quietly started rummaging for my clothes.

"Are you sneaking out on me?" Lauren's soft syrupy voice pierced the silence.

I turned toward her with the ends of my socks in my hand.

"I don't know if that's possible considering I live here."

"Come back to bed." She smoothed the sheets and I hesitated for a second, but I ignored her request and continued to search for my clothes.

"Kate, come back to bed."

I stopped but I couldn't look right at her. "I've asked myself every day over the years why you? Why not someone who wanted me back? Who was available? Why did this only happen with you? Unrequited love," I muttered. "I'm a prisoner of unrequited love. I'm trapped. If you weren't married and we dated back in college, it probably would have been great, but just like anything else, it would have flamed out and I'd be free. But I'm perpetually trapped in these what-ifs with you and last night I created a whole new series. The worst part is that those what-ifs break you down and you conjure up memories in your head that never even happened."

"It wouldn't have flamed out."

A calmness settled over me and I closed my eyes. "There's a pain that I feel deep in my ribs. It pulls on every last nerve ending; it's visceral. Sometimes I can actually see it coming off me in waves. You are the single solitary reason for that pain. Please keep your hands and legs inside the roller coaster at all times and keep your thoughts to yourself. I beg you. If you care for me at all, you'll never say that again."

"Kate—"

"Never again." I reached for my shirt. "What am I to you? You wind me up and watch me go? Are you having fun?"

"I was until you woke up this morning and decided that running from this would be the solution instead of talking."

"We're talking right now." I ignored her comment as I shrugged into my jeans. She could keep the bra and panties as souvenirs. "This was a mistake."

"Kate, stop. I loved you then. I love you now. Through all of this, I never stopped loving you. It was never unrequited. If that's what you told yourself to make it easier, to make it hurt a little less, then I understand but it was never unrequited."

"Bullshit."

"Who has a revisionist history now?"

"You lied," I said so quietly that I thought she didn't hear.

"No, I didn't!" She practically shouted. "I tried to tell you the other day. I tried to tell you in college, but I couldn't do that to you. You had just gotten into law school…" She put her hand over her heart and her eyes started to water. "You're not the only one who has thought about what-ifs over these past years."

"Why are you still lying to me?"

"Go to the library."

"Are you kicking me out of my own house?"

"Go to the third floor. In the history section, the second case, on the bottom of the shelf, you'll find an orange book on Minimalism that sticks out like a sore thumb. Find it."

"I don't want to play games with you."

"This isn't a game." She looked at me intently. "Find the book."

After she dressed and left my house, I sat on my hands and looked at the current state of my bedroom. I was transported back to my college days and the precise moments after we had been intimate and she left my apartment, an empty feeling settled into my chest, but it was different this time; it felt worse. I closed my eyes and inhaled deeply. All I could smell was Lauren. I brought my hands to my head and started to cry. I was infuriated for letting her in once again. I knew deep down that in doing so, I had effectively ruined any chance of ever moving on with another living soul. That I could deal with, I had for the last fifteen years, but the anger that I felt toward myself for kicking her out that morning was unbearable.

I left the house with my work keys in my hand, jumped into the car and drove to the library. I unlocked the doors and jogged up the steps, two at a time, to the third floor. No matter how hard I tried, I couldn't move fast enough. I made a beeline to the history section and sitting on the second case at the bottom of the shelf was a book that had mocked me for my entire college career and now held some sort of powder keg about to go off. I picked it up off of the shelf and looked down at the cover with a blank expression. I closed my eyes and slowly opened it, waiting with baited breath for my world to explode into a thousand tiny pieces.

When I opened the book, there were a series of notes folded in half. I opened the first note and it was Lauren's unmistakable handwriting. The first note was dated a year after I left town.

i miss you all the time.

There was a note for every year that I was away.

i can't let you go. My marriage is all but over, but we keep going. We both know the reason... i'm sorry.

Do you know how many times i've looked you up online? Countless, but today i finally found something. You're as beautiful as i remember.

i have a daughter, her name is Abbie. You'd love her.

i've written you dozens of letters, but i never finish them. i've picked up the phone thousands of times, dialed your work number, let reception pick it up but i always hang up the phone.

is this healthy? i told myself to stop coming to write you these notes. i guess all of my other alternatives, writing you, calling you, coming to see you... This may be the best option.

Someone moved the book! i got so excited. i raced around the library looking for you. You're not the only one who has a great set of eyes for books that are out of place. i want to tell you that i didn't cry when i came to the realization that it wasn't you, but i can't. i still think about you all the time. i play a million what-ifs around in my mind.

i bought the Steam Bean. i daydream about you walking through the doors one day and i really need to stop doing that.

Roses are red, violets are blue, i love you, Kate. i love you.

10 years... This would have been our 'tin' anniversary, which is completely appropriate. A tin man... Woman... if i only had a heart... You've taken mine, and i don't know what to do any longer. i think this will be the last note.

Every year I come back to the library and stick notes in this book. i usually do it around the same time, when we kissed. i'm a month late. When the day came around and i didn't come to the library, it was incredibly difficult. i did my best to stay away, but i could only last a month. i couldn't think of a way for us to be together at the time and since you've left, i've come up with 1,000,001 different scenarios. isn't that funny? i knew whatever decision i made would hurt you tremendously... i just never realized how badly it would hurt me.

i'm stuck. i miss you. i want you. i love you and you probably moved on a long time ago.

When does this end?

You're home... and you hate me.

The last note was dated only a couple of weeks ago.
Kate,
i'm not the original book bandit, but when i had nothing, i had this. it was an outlet for me during some very dark moments, but above all else, it was a connection to you...and i couldn't let it go.

i'm in love with you. i've been in love with you from the moment we met and every breath that has followed. You're my best friend. i know that i've hurt you. i hurt myself.

i'm going to say something that you won't like, but it's true...

i wouldn't change anything that has happened between us or the decisions that we made to get to this moment because i have Abbie, the shop, and a life that i really love.

i wouldn't change it because you have Jack, the library, and a life which i think you're really starting to love again.

The only missing piece in my life is you. You asked me to try fifteen years ago and i should have said yes.

i'm asking you to try now.

Please don't make the same mistake that i did.

Please give us a chance.

Love always,
Lauren

The book slipped from my hands and tumbled haphazardly to the floor. When I picked it up, another note came loose. It was dated a few weeks after I left Renfrew. I read the four words and blinked in confusion. I read it a second, third, and fourth time but the letters felt like they belonged to some language that I didn't understand. I inspected the curves and although I wanted to be wrong, there was no mistaking Lauren's handwriting.
i lost the baby.

I stood there stunned, the last few weeks of our relationship in college flashed through my mind. The memories and emotions swirled and when it finally came to an end, I thought I was going to be sick.
I ran from the library.

CHAPTER FORTY-SIX

I burst into the Steam Bean just before it closed. The commotion caused Lauren to turn around, when she did, the apprehension in her eyes was unmistakable.

"Where are the girls?" I asked quickly.

"Playing in the back."

I walked behind the counter and stopped within a few feet of her. "You were pregnant."

She nodded.

"You were pregnant..." I said again. I had said so much over the past year because of my pain, but never those words. "You knew the last night we were together. That's why you didn't want to leave." She said nothing but the look on her face confirmed it and I paced. "That's why you told me not to forget. You were going to leave him but you found out you were pregnant."

"Yes." She finally spoke, and the agony in that one word made my stomach drop and I stood still.

Lauren's affirmation was the piece to the puzzle that I had been missing for fifteen years. I opened my mouth again, but nothing came out.

"I never picked him. The circumstance did. Drew didn't find out about us. I told him about us and then I found out I was pregnant, and everything changed. I didn't tell him about the pregnancy initially, but I couldn't hide losing the baby."

My conversation with Drew flashed in my mind. It finally dawned on me. His words and the vitriol behind them, *you have no idea the lives you've ruined.* "He blames me."

Her sigh confirmed it.

"Why?"

"He thought the stress of you leaving caused it to happen." She shook her head softly. "I've never once thought that. Not once. Sometimes things just happen."

"Why didn't you say something to me over this last year?"

"I never talked about it with him. I didn't talk about it with anyone for a very long time. I held it close to me because it was so many different things from that period of my life. Loss was not going to be what brought us back together. It couldn't be the reason, Kate."

"If you would have told me fifteen years ago… If I had known, I never would have left."

"Which is exactly why I didn't tell you. What were you going to do? Help me raise someone else's child? Undo all of the plans that you had for yourself?"

"But I didn't want those plans… I wanted us."

"I couldn't do that to you."

"Lauren, I was happiest here. Why didn't you leave him after?"

"It connected us. If it wasn't for that connection we never would've had Abbie. But after she was born, it was gone."

"Why didn't you contact me?"

"I thought about it a thousand times, but I never heard from you. I thought you were happy."

I wanted to drop to my knees. The blinding sting of the first few tears didn't surprise me.

"You're crying."

I wiped furiously at my eyes. "I have resented you for fifteen years. I have acted like a petulant child for the last year and this changes everything... But we're right back where we started, don't you see? We lost all that time."

"You keep looking at what we didn't have, but you're failing to see everything we do have that makes us great."

I wanted to argue. I wanted to put up a fight. I wanted to justify the loss, but I couldn't. She was right. "I'm so sorry that I wasn't here for you."

"Everything happens for a reason, including you coming back to Renfrew and last night."

"This morning..." I shook my head in disgust. "I handled it like someone who had just gotten her heart broken. Please know that I am not justifying my actions. I would give anything to go back and redo this morning and give it the proper ending. You didn't deserve it. As soon as I woke up, I could only think about myself. I didn't stop for a second to think about you, how last night impacted you, or how you were feeling." I held out my hands palms up. "And one of the worst things in all of this is that I lied to Jack."

She tilted her head.

"I told her that if I found someone who I was meant to be with, I would hold on with both hands and never let go..." I exhaled. "You've been reaching for my hands for the last year and I was too caught up in my own hurt to reach back." The next words rushed out. "I loved you so much in college."

"I know." She reached for my hands and squeezed them.

"I never said it, but I did. It has always been you. It's always going to be you."

"*Us.* It's always going to be us."

"I love you." I wrapped my arms around her, pulling her as close as she could get, and whispered the words over and over. For the first time in fifteen years, I felt free. I pulled back fractionally. "Now what?"

She placed a light kiss upon my lips. "They lived happily ever after."

"Jack's going to kill us."

"We'll cross that bridge when we get to it." Her warm smile pressed into the underside of my jaw. "Are you ever going to tell me about the benefits of the book club?"

"I believe you experienced many of those benefits last night. But if you need a reminder, I'm free this evening, and the one after that, and the one after that…"

"And all the ones after that." She wrapped her arms around my neck and kissed me until her warmth started to spread.

"Mom!" Abbie's excited voice rang out. The kissing instantly stopped and we both froze.

"Mom?" Jack's voice wasn't as excited, probably because she had just come to the realization that this would severely hamper her future wedding plans.

"I think we just crossed that bridge," Lauren softly whispered.

I shook my head, pulled her into a hug and I knew that I was never going to let go. "Just five more minutes."

EPILOGUE

Six years later…

I placed my coffee cup on the nightstand and sighed loudly into the sanctity of our bedroom. "I think I'm ready to know…"

She put down her book, turned to me, her glasses hung just off the tip of her nose. "Twenty-one years later and you want to know today."

"Well, I put a ring on it and since you didn't bolt after our wooden anniversary, I figured you're probably going to stick it out with me."

"Stick it out?"

"Knock on wood."

She leaned over and kissed the corner of my mouth. "I'm not going anywhere." She pushed herself back and got out of bed.

"Liar!"

She opened the medicine cabinet, pulled out her little black case and sat back in bed. She slowly unzipped the case while she wiggled her eyebrows in anticipation. She removed a nondescript bottle with an ink dropper. She unscrewed the top and held it out for me to smell.

I inhaled slowly until it reached my toes. "*Mmmm*, that's half of you. What is it?"

"Are you sure?"

"Rip that Band-Aid right off."

"Honeysuckle. I mix it into the lavender."

She pulled out another bottle, one I recognized, and sprayed a small amount on her wrist. She mixed a drop from the honeysuckle and rubbed the concoction just behind her ear. She leaned forward and I inhaled deeply once again. My favorite smell, Lauren. I moved away fractionally and leaned back. "You put honeysuckle in the coffee?"

"If I ever do, I'll make sure to bump up your life insurance policy first."

"I don't understand."

"It's poisonous, you'd get sick. The scent I wear is lavender and honeysuckle, but you get a little bit of lavender honey in your coffee. It was the closest I could get."

"You've been drugging me since the outset."

"You love it."

I rolled my eyes, but she could see right through me. "I love you, but I'm cancelling my life insurance on Monday morning. Can't take any chances."

She laughed, pulled herself into my lap, and wrapped her arms around my neck. "What do you want to do today?"

"Ravage you…but we need to wait for the kids to wake up first so I can kick them out of the house. Rain check?"

"Absolutely. What do you want to do before then?"

I untangled her arms from my neck. "Lift your arms up." She did and I pulled off her cotton shirt and tossed it to the side.

"I thought you wanted to wait until later."

"The ravaging can wait. I can try and be quiet if you can."

"You know I can't."

I released a soft hum-sigh and smiled. "I know. I count that blessing everyday…but try."

And we did.